ISBN 978-1-59433-063-6

Library of Congress Catalog Card Number: 2007938769

Copyright 2007 by Don Porter
—First Edition—

All rights reserved, including the right of reproduction in any form, or by any mechanical or electronic means including photocopying or recording, or by any information storage or retrieval system, in whole or in part in any form, and in any case not without the written permission of the author and publisher.

Cover Illustration ©2007 Hal Gage
Cover Design by Gage Photo Graphics, Anchorage, Alaska

Manufactured in the United States of America.

Dedication

The Dealership is dedicated to the staff and management of KITV, the ABC network affiliate for Hawaii. I spent fifteen wonderful years as a member of that family and was happy to go to work each and every day. Every person in every department was a consummate professional, and we worked together in the best tradition of Aloha. I can't name names because the list would run off the page, and if I started there'd be no place to stop. Many of you will recognize places and situations in this book.

Thanks, folks.

Other Books by Don Porter

Deadly Detail Hard Cover
ISBN 1-59058-191-1

Deadly Detail Soft Cover, Large Print,
ISBN 1-59058-192-X

Happy Hour
ISBN 0-9706712-5-3

Yukon Murders
ISBN 13 978-0-9706712-9-5
ISBN 10 0-9706712-9-6

All are set in Alaska, All feature Alex Price, bush pilot.

Don G Porter

a hui ho

Acknowledgements

If it's still legal, I'd like to quote Jesus Christ as recorded in Matthew 7:3. He said, "Why beholdest thou the mote that is in thy brother's eye, but considerest not the beam that is in thine own eye?

Clearly he was speaking to authors who are trying to edit their own material. It can't be done. The beam in thine own eye is invisible, but your fellow writers and editors can spot the motes from across the room. If a mistake gets past them, you can bet that readers will find it and complain.

In this book the final word belonged to Evan Swensen of Publication Consultants and editors Marthy Johnson and Rebecca Goodrich.

But, before Evan and editors took their whacks at me a good many motes and some beams were spotted by my cadre of editors and fellow authors. The editors who bring a touch of professionalism to my scribblings are Joann Condit and C.J. Seidlitz. I don't sign my name without consulting one or both of them.

Fellow authors who read and comment include Ivan Pierce, William Marsik, Gale Gill, and Marjorie Dobbin. Three of my sons are writers and will struggle through my stuff when I can catch them. That's Don F., Ronald, and Gregory.

And the best thing I've ever done was marrying Deborah who is truly a help mate.

Foreword

The Dealership is intrigue and humor with a special flavor of Hawaii. Many people see the islands only as a tourist destination, but *The Dealership* takes us on a journey revealing even to locals. Don Porter's Hawaii comes alive with the nuances of modern culture mixed with historical influence. His Hawaii becomes fertile ground for a compelling mystery. Along the way we get a Hawaiian history lesson—a true feeling for the place, its people, and our cultural idiosyncrasies—and by the way, 8 FatFat 8 really exists.

I have known Don as a television engineer but much more of the man is revealed through his *The Dealership*. Porter's colorful background includes years of adventure in Alaska. As a bush pilot he encountered such challenging and dangerous conditions that life and death decisions became commonplace. He is not unlike the protagonist in *The Dealership*, having to think and act judiciously and with speed to avoid disaster. On the surface is an unassuming fellow, but his wry wit leaps off the pages of *The Dealership*. His descriptive talents put you in the moment, right there in every scene. Even in the midst of action, his characters ring true with the absurdity that so often accompanies high drama .

If I had been aware that Don Porter were such a word merchant, I would have made a play for him to be a producer in the news department, at the risk of making an enemy of the folks in engineering.

Enuff already! Read it for yourself.

Gary Sprinkle
Television Anchor, Honolulu, Hawaii

Chapter One

"Hey, Dick, don't you miss the old Hotel Street?" George asked. He was standing by the window, hands in pockets, broad Hawaiian suntanned brow furrowed.

"Shall I tell you the truth, or say what's politically correct?"

"Truth might be a refreshing change, if it's still legal."

I wandered over and stood beside George, looking down from our thirty-sixth-floor office at the boarded-up remains of what used to be the seedier core of Honolulu's personality, the center of drugs, prostitution, and booze. Clubs, bars, and sex shops had windows covered by plywood, plastered with closure and eviction notices instead of the girlie pictures and come-on slogans that used to line the street. The survivors that were still open, mostly restaurants, seemed to be peeking out of burrows. The effect was like pictures you've seen of war-torn streets in Europe after an air raid—ruin and desolation.

If you've been through Honolulu in the last sixty years, or seen any of the old movies, you probably would recognize the sign, now dark and peeling, over the Hubba Hubba Club. That dispensary of soft-core sexual innuendo met every criterion for a National Monument, except approval.

The heavy dark curtains that always seemed to have a few gaps so that strollers on the sidewalk could glimpse the strippers under the spotlights were now covered by unpainted plywood. The Hubba Hubba Club, like most of its neighbors, had been busted for one or another of the technical "crimes" that locals and tourists used to flock there to enjoy.

I turned away from the window and walked back to my desk. George spent another minute watching the bright sunshine shimmer off the Waianae Mountains and the crush of marine traffic in Honolulu Harbor. A 747 lifted off the Reef Runway and screamed in protest while its pilots tore it away from our tropical paradise and banked toward the rain and misery of a Seattle winter. George left the window (reluctantly, I thought), and shuffled back to his desk, picking up the file of chaos that represented our latest client.

George leaned elbows on his blotter, dug his sausage-sized fingers into his thick, curly black hair, and went back to studying the folder. He hunched his linebacker's shoulders that threatened to rip his outrageous crimson-and-gold, hibiscus-printed aloha shirt, and was either reading diligently or taking a nap.

I didn't need to read the folder, I had that sucker memorized, but it didn't help. I watched the sunlight creep into our west-facing window and turn the orchids in the window box into miniature Chinese lanterns.

One of the problems with our new client was that none of us—including Sally herself—was sure that she'd be around to pay our fee. When she sat in the client's chair, crossed three feet of delectable bare legs under a short yellow sundress, and tried to explain her situation, I listened for thirty seconds, went into overload, and took notes. You've read in the daily papers about her husband's death, and you know that police are looking for the murderer. The cops are concentrating on the *who*, but Sally was worried about the *why*.

She and Darren had held all properties jointly and operated the businesses as partners, and Darren's murder did appear to be a professional execution. Darren's body was found sprawled face down on the cabin floor of their yacht with a single .38 slug in the back of his head. It had occurred to Sally that anyone interested in removing Darren probably had sights set on her too—figuratively speaking, I hope.

It was Sally's contention that the cops have more than they can handle trying to deal with crimes that have already happened, and don't pay much attention to theoretical crimes that might happen in the future. As the possible victim of a future crime, she was hiring private detectives to reverse those priorities.

I guessed from George's expression that he and I were having the same interesting thoughts about bodyguarding Sally—almost platinum blonde hair brushing her shoulders, a slender face you expect to see only in movies, blue eyes the color of waves just before they break. But that department was already covered. What she was hiring us to do was investigate business associates, employees, anyone we could think of who might have had or imagined a motive to kill Darren.

Hirosha, Sally's chauffeur, stood in the office door during the interview, effectively blocking the door, possibly expecting our receptionist

Chapter One

to burst in shooting wildly with a submachine gun. I had to agree that Sally didn't need more bodyguarding. Hiro was five foot six, but in every direction, like the little teapot, short and stout. He wasn't obese; he was a giant who had neglected to grow tall. He had a square head, a bush of black hair, and a demeanor that could explain the expression, *inscrutable Oriental*. His black uniform jacket must have been tailor made, but his muscles kept it flapping open when he moved so you could see the .38 in his shoulder holster most of the time.

Our client chairs are wooden but with leather-upholstered seats and backs. Clients are comfortable but not tempted to go to sleep. Sally sat there crossing and recrossing those marvelous long legs of hers, but it wasn't a Sharon Stone ploy, it was just a nervous habit. She certainly was nervous.

Before she sat down she scooted the chair away from the thirty-sixth-floor window so that her back was against the beige plaster wall, but she still kept glancing over her shoulder, apparently expecting an assassin to burst through the wall. When a client is nervous, it's a good time to discuss our fee.

I swept an expansive arm around the office, which contained our two desks, the separate table with the computer, fax machine, and copier, and the row of filing cabinets across the back wall. My gesture included Maggie, the receptionist in the outer office, by implication, but did not indicate that most of the files were empty, the one notable content being my laundry bag, which I intended to drop off after work.

"All of our facilities," I said, "are at your disposal for two thousand dollars per day ..." and when she didn't wince I added, "plus expenses." Still no wince, so I said, "Our usual retainer is ten thousand dollars in advance."

She didn't even bat the mascara, just leaned over and scooped up the yellow leather purse that was sitting on the carpet next to yellow high heels. She had put both feet on the carpet for that maneuver, but immediately crossed her knees again, extracted a checkbook and a gold pen from the purse, and wrote out the check: "Pay to the order of Payne and Clark Detective Agency, $10,000." Signed: Sally K. Chambers.

I was happy to note that the Chambers on the check is the same Chambers as the Chambers Auto Group. If you've bought a car, new or used, anywhere in Hawaii in the last ten years, you had the option of buying it from Chambers; they seem to have car lots in every

The Dealership

city on the islands. If you've made it from the Honolulu Airport to downtown, you've already passed two of their dealerships.

One of the things that surprised me when we started compiling our file was that they don't handle any one particular make. It's Chambers Ford in one town, Chambers Chevrolet in the next, and each dealership handles two or three brands, like maybe, "Chambers Chevrolet, Datsun, and Hyundai." It made perfect sense in the old days to see a Ford-Lincoln-Mercury dealer, cars made by the same company, but it seemed to me that Chambers was mixing brands by fiercely competing manufacturers. If they wanted to move into a new town that already had a Ford and a Chevy dealer, no problem; they became Chambers Chrysler, Jeep, and whatever else was available.

I really wasn't gouging Sally on the fee. Our little two-room office suite cost twelve thousand dollars a month. Maggie at the reception desk cost thirty-five hundred mostly for reading romance novels and buffing her nails. Don't come running to apply for Maggie's job; her take-home pay is little more than half of that. The rest is taxes and insurance that Hawaii mandates for all employees.

We do a good business, if that's not an oxymoron. One of our chief sources of income is skip tracing, in partnership with some mainland contacts. A lot of people think they can skip out on mainland warrants by flying to the middle of the Pacific Ocean. When they land here, we meet them, drape an orchid lei around their necks, kiss their cheeks, and handcuff them. We have our fair share of the routine, pain-in-the-anatomy cases, but still there are months when George and I would be illegally paying ourselves less than minimum wage if we were hourly employees.

We should make a distinction between people who live in Hawaii and Hawaiians as a race. George, with 99.9% Hawaiian genes, was a distinct minority. When Hawaii's agriculture ramped up, labor was imported. In turn, Japanese, Filipinos, Chinese, and various South Sea islanders were brought in to work in the cane fields and later pineapple plantations. Each group rebelled at the slave labor conditions and got their children educated to become doctors and lawyers. The end result of that revolution is that today the sugar cane fields are things of the past. Most of the pineapple business is following close behind.

South America, and Southeast Asia, where wages are still ten cents to the Hawaiian dollar have taken over the agriculture. In Hawaii today, slave labor is confined to the maids in the hotels, and maybe the private detectives who try to find whatever is missing and hope

Chapter One

not to get shot in domestic violence cases. If your idea of domestic violence is a husband and wife slapping each other around, then you do not want to know about paradise, where domestic violence includes shotguns, dynamite, and arson, mostly thanks to the mix of races and cultures.

The sun passed the window box orchids and spilled onto the maroon carpet. The clash of colors was startling, but they were bright, and that's the main requirement in Hawaii. Fortunately, we would be headed for a cocktail before the sun reached George's florescent shirt. Oahu is a tropical island, so a little thirst is to be expected, and the time had come to stimulate and consult the gray cells. My mind was churning, but it was an exercise in futility. Sally's potential murderer was probably in our file, but that only added to the frustration; the file was too big.

Sherlock Holmes said, "Eliminate the impossible and whatever is left must be true, no matter how improbable." So far we had eliminated twenty-nine impossibles: twenty-seven off the island and two already dead themselves. That left 947 improbables.

We'd have been happy to work on Sally's case all night if we had a lead, but since we didn't, we locked up the office at five-fifteen. Maggie, as usual, had escaped the moment the second hand on the wall clock ticked to five. Her chair was kicked back like the starting blocks in a race, and the Harlequin romance she'd been reading lay spine up, the only paper on her desk.

We retrieved our cars from the basement parking lot, bulled through the rush hour crush, and met at the bar, 8 Fat Fat 8, on Beretania Street, mainly because that's where our agendas were going to diverge for the evening. From there, I'd turn down Keeaumoku Street toward Waikiki, and George would go on out King Street, pick up the freeway, and head for the beach house on Kalanianaole Highway. George had a new romantic interest, and that just naturally led toward the beach. I hadn't met his new paramour yet and George didn't seem to want to talk about her beyond the fact that her name was Monica and she was an actress. He was silent about just what she acted in, and I had the impression she's not the sort of girl one takes home to mother.

I was singularly between romantic interests at the moment. Betty had caught a bad case of island fever and had to go back to Des Moines. Island fever isn't caused by a virus, and in fact, is not a physical disease, although a severe case can have bad physical effects. It's a psychological problem, maybe a form of claustrophobia. The victim suddenly pictures his or her position on a tiny rock in the middle of a large ocean and starts scrambling for life preservers.

The way Betty put it was that she needed to be in a place where you can drive more than an hour in one direction. I pointed out that you can drive as long as you wish on Oahu, but it is true that if you drive more than three hours, you will be back where you started. My persuasive powers failed; Betty went from nervous to terrified. At that point, you're dealing with a psychosis or a phobia, one of those conditions that you don't reason with or talk people out of. We held a tearful goodbye wake, drinking Tropical Itches at Stinger Ray's in the Honolulu airport, and Betty dashed down that jetway like Dorothy leaving the land of Oz.

George and I are not really habitués of 8 Fat Fat 8, but we stop there often enough that Cy gave us a wave and had our drinks mixed before we got to the bar. It's not Cheers. I doubt Cy knew our names; he just knew us as *Gin and Tonic and Rum and Coke*, but still it is a warm feeling.

The bar is an island of light in the back of the room past twenty atmosphere-lit booths. The room is pleasantly air conditioned and it smells more like appetizers than spilled beer. The two couples who occupied booths had camped in the darkest corners so it seemed polite not to notice them.

George found a stool that didn't wobble, put one foot up on the brass rail, sampled his gin. "Think we should start checking out employees?"

My stool wasn't so stable, so I put both feet on the rail. The rum went straight to the thirst. "All five hundred of them? She'll die of old age before that gets us anywhere."

"Good point, but at two thousand dollars per day we won't have to worry about the rent anymore."

"It will be hard to collect if she gets murdered in the meantime. That is a real possibility, and if she does get bumped off, it will be our fault. Damn, can you imagine anyone wanting to kill that gorgeous lady?"

"Well, not in any usual way," George admitted. He took another sip and his eyes glazed like he was thinking, but I doubted he was thinking about solutions to our problem.

I tried to steer George back toward reality. "Business contacts would be just as tough. There must be three hundred regulars, but maybe one of them is the Mafia."

Cy brought a saucer-sized plate with chunks of Fat Fat special

Chapter One

chicken and set it between us. We nodded our thanks and each grabbed a chunk.

George swallowed chicken, washed it down, "Maybe we should be checking customers, maybe he sold someone a lemon."

"That's a brilliant suggestion." I rushed to finish my first piece of chicken. It had been marinated in soy sauce and several spices, positively addictive, and one of the main perks of living in Hawaii. Six pieces almost covered the plate and I was aiming for a three-and-three split. If I dawdled, George would make it a four-two split without noticing. "Chambers Group sells two hundred cars a day—how many months shall we go back?"

We each picked up a second chunk and sipped and savored in silence for a moment. I was pretty safe now—with only two left on the plate the sharing protocol was obvious. People were beginning to drift in for after-work transfusions. A couple of Filipino businessmen wearing jackets and ties marched in and scraped back stools two spaces down, friendly but not intrusive. We exchanged nods, although we didn't know them, we just recognized each other as belonging in the neighborhood. Cy was handing them drinks while they were still testing stools.

Four young guys wearing work shirts and jeans came in, turned on the light over the dartboard, and started playing. That is one disadvantage of Fat Fat. The dart range is just inside the front door. You have to survive that, then work past the booths to get to the bar. The noise level was starting to rise, but no one had plugged the jukebox.

Nominally 8 Fat Fat 8 is a Chinese bar, and Cy is Chinese, taller and more slender than most Eurasians with a noble face that was chiseled rather than molded. The clientele, like Hawaii itself, is a mixture of Pacific Rim. George and I were two minorities, George the only Hawaiian and me the only haole. I guess that's not technically true, because *haole* is a Polynesian word meaning "not Polynesian," but the mix is so confused that you almost have to be Irish to qualify as a haole.

"What I want to do is get a look at the scene of the crime," I said. "If we knew why Darren was on his yacht, we'd know who killed him."

"Not necessarily." George paused for another sip. "If he was there for the obvious reason, then the murderer is our lovely client, and if so, why did she hire us?"

"Do you really think a guy who was married to Sally would be screwing around?"

17

George shrugged his over-abundant shoulders, "Hey, if it can happen to Kathy Lee Gifford, it can happen to anyone. I think there's something fundamentally wrong with the Y chromosome, left over from jungle survival, like the prehensile tail."

"Well, you should know about that, but the possibility hadn't occurred to Sally. Besides, Frank Gifford was set up, pure and simple. Some tabloid planted a bimbo on him and caught him in a weak moment."

"Yeah, poor guy." George was nodding with that far away look again. "We should all have such lousy luck. Want to get a court order to visit the crime scene?"

"Nah, the cops are through with the yacht; they're just a little slow taking down their tape. Meet you on the dock around eight?"

"Around nine," George decided.

Floralitta bustled in, a happy smile on her china-doll face and a friendly nod to each of us, as if she were glad to be at work. She slipped behind the bar and exchanged her jacket for a tiny green apron that she tied around her 18-inch waist. Interesting, because it was eighty degrees outside and seventy-five inside, also because whenever Floralitta moves it's intrinsically interesting. She shrugged a yard of black silk tresses into a snood and took her order pad out to brave the dartboard.

I reached for the last chunk of chicken without looking, and my fingers found an empty plate; the last piece was halfway to George's mouth. He stopped and gave me what was an apologetic look, for George. At least, he raised his eyebrows.

"You go right ahead," I told him. "In half an hour I'll be eating a steak at Stuart Anderson's and you'll be stuck in traffic halfway to Maunalua Bay."

George shrugged his shoulders again—he seemed to be doing a lot of that lately—and popped the chicken into his mouth.

I dropped the laundry at Al Phillips The Cleaners in Ala Moana Shopping Center, and drove over to Stuart Anderson's at Ward Center; but I didn't have a steak. I switched to the prime rib at the last moment. The rib was superb, I was cutting a medium rare slab two inches thick with my fork. The baked potato was as smooth as Sally's cheek and smothered with all the good stuff, the Caesar salad was jet-fresh, and the mini-skirted waitresses kept reminding me that life is fun. Problem was that I couldn't enjoy it; my mind was churning over the probability that someone was out there planning to murder Sally.

I watched the sunset over the Kewalo Basin boat harbor where

Chapter One

the tourists were lining up for dinner cruises. The sun made the usual explosion of orange streaks that turn the ocean to magenta with winking orange diamonds, but it faded fast and turned red. Blood red, to be specific, like Sally's blood if someone shot her.

I turned my back on the windows and tried the bar where I made a serious dent in a bottle of Captain Morgan's rum, but it didn't help. All I really saw was the image of Sally squirming around in our client's chair. How the heck do you investigate a murder that hasn't happened yet?

Chapter Two

The best thing about Hawaii's marinas is that there aren't any seagulls. Things aren't dotted with white splotches, and no sudden splats of white mush fall on your head or shoulders. I parked the Jaguar on the gravel median between docks and leaned against it, enjoying the morning sunshine and the eighty-degree trade winds while I waited for George. The Jag is the SV6 sedan, black, not flashy, just a good practical car. George's baby blue BMW convertible is snappier, and it suits him.

Both cars belonged to the company, and both were purchased from the Chambers Auto Group. That is one advantage of being in business. When you do have a good year, specifically the year we found the loot from the Hong Kong diamond heist aboard the *King Midas*, you have the option of paying taxes or having business expenses. George had wanted a Lamborghini, but it wasn't that good a year.

The Ala Wai Yacht Harbor consists of a U–shaped drive, the Waikiki Yacht Club at the end, and a couple of hundred yachts, all sizes, shapes, and income brackets, bobbing between wooden walkways around the U. A lot of people lived aboard their boats and had made their slips homey with bougainvillea over the gates, flowers in pots and clinging to the edge of the gravel, even a few papaya trees bearing fruit or promise.

I was looking inland through a forest of masts, optimistically watching for George. I was facing the back of the cubic-block Ilikai Hotel with its tropical atrium and swimming pool on a lanai a couple of floors up, and the mostly glass monolith of the Prince Kuhio Hotel on my left. George was only fifteen minutes late, not bad for him, but I punished him by turning my back on the entrance, leaning across the top of the car, and looking the other way toward the

Chapter Two

rock jetty, the miniscule beach, and the surf breaking on the reef two hundred yards off shore.

A dozen surfers were already out, riding a four-foot swell outside the reef. Waves broke on the reef with a crash and a fountain of spray, and most surfers prudently ended their rides before they got to the reef. Just to the right of the surfers between a couple of buoys, the entrance to the harbor was cut through the reef so the waves rolled right on in. Occasionally a surfer who was having a good ride couldn't resist entering the channel and risking dismemberment by an outbound yacht rather than lose his wave.

I had watched several surfers take the chance, but none had paid the price, when the gravel crunched beside me, and George climbed out of the BMW. He was wearing an aloha shirt, fifteen shades of shocking green with scarlet hibiscus peeking out of a jungle motif. I was wearing an aloha shirt, too, of course—it's mandatory, but I tend to pick colors you can look at without sunglasses. I also wasn't sporting George's smug smile.

"Have a nice night?" I asked.

"Tolerable."

I wasn't prying, and George was not going to volunteer details; we're a bit past the kiss-and-tell stage. I was just checking to see that no calamities had occurred. We turned our attention to the yacht, and she well deserved it. We strolled across the gravel drive.

"Nice tub," George said. He was eyeing her with that same covetous expression, wrinkled forehead and narrowed eyes, that he had worn while I was convincing him that we could not afford the Lamborghini.

The *Sally C* was understated elegance, polished and reflecting the sunshine, with enough mast to string a high-tension power line, sail furled and covered by a blue plastic zipper bag. The entrance to the dock was guarded by a chainlink fence and a gate blocked with both a padlock and yellow "Police line, do not cross" tape. The next slip on our left was friendlier with only a three-foot white picket fence. Rather than defy the police line, we stepped over the picket fence, around the end of the chainlink, and sidestepped along the top of a wooden retaining wall, backsides hanging over the water, fingers through the fence like a couple of monkeys in a cage. We made it without getting dunked and strolled out onto the wooden dock between the *Sally C* and the *Wander Lust*.

There wasn't any manufacturer's nameplate on the *Sally C*; I guess it didn't need one. Yachting people would recognize it. I knew from

The Dealership

Sally's list of assets that it was made in Belgium, a fifty-six-foot Swan with a one-point-one-million-dollar price tag. Like our cars, it was a legitimate business expense, necessary to entertain clients. Except for a blue racing stripe, and a deck that I think was mahogany, the ship was seamless, sparkling white. There didn't appear to be any cabin, just a one-foot rise down the center with portholes practically on the deck. Mostly it was sleek and looked as if it were going fifty miles an hour tied up at the dock.

We stepped over a low rail onto the boat, crossed ten feet of dark, polished hardwood deck, and George led the way down a few steps to open the door at the back of the cabin. We both saw the tripwire on the third step just as George stepped on it and we heard the click.

I hollered, "Run," but I needn't have. George was already passing me, back up the stairs and we were both in the air, diving off the stern into the water when the explosion ripped the ship. The sound of that explosion was a live thing that shook me when it shuddered past. Time stopped while I waited to hit the water, boosted along by flying glass and splinters of wood. The door George had been reaching for passed me and hit the water ahead with a splash.

I made a splash of my own and bumped into George, already six feet down and clawing to go deeper. The first shock of water felt cold for a moment, but I was distracted by what appeared to be an underwater rainstorm, lots of glass, a brass doorknob, a polished brass skillet, a frame that might have been half a chair.

George went by on his way up, and the rain had stopped, so I followed him. When we broke the surface and got through gasping and spitting, the yacht didn't look much different than before except that the subliminal cabin was gone. We dog-paddled past the door and around the flotsam. It's not that we aren't both good swimmers, but with clothes and shoes on, you don't try for any Olympic style. A rubber tire hung down from the dock by a rope, George clambered up and I was right behind him. We sprawled on the wooden dock and it felt warm and wonderful.

"You okay?" George asked.

"Better than you, I think." I reached over and removed a three-inch glass arrowhead with its tip stuck in his back.

"Ouch, what did you do that for?" He was looking over his shoulder and I showed him the shard.

"Want me to put it back?"

Chapter Two

People were running across the lot toward us; a siren cranked up over by the Ilikai.

"Bad place to be," George said. We slipped back into the water, under the dock and paddled around the stern of the *Wander Lust*. The next slip was vacant so we swam underwater to the next dock, and that turned out to be quite a project with wet clothes and shoes dragging us down. We worked along under that dock to the retaining wall and climbed up, using the wall and a piling for a ladder.

Quite a few people had gathered at the police line, and more were running, but everyone was concentrating on the *Sally C* and had their backs to us. We sat on the edge of the dock, dripping and trying to look innocent.

"I need a drink." George was looking down at his hands and wiping blood off on his wet pants.

"Sorry, I don't have one with me."

"There's a half bottle of tequila at the beach house and some dry clothes."

"Want to squish past that crowd to the cars?" I asked. "We could pretend we'd just been out for a swim."

A police cruiser came screeching and flashing down the drive and stopped just short of the crowd. Two cops jumped out, and for want of something constructive to do, they started trying to move the crowd back away from the fence. The gawkers were still hoping to see mangled bodies, so they were making a fuss.

"Now," George decided. "We'll take the convertible. Don't open the doors, just step over."

We strolled as nonchalantly as one can with clothes and hair dripping and shoes squishing. Another cop car came racing down the lane, siren blaring, and slid to a stop beside the first. Two more cops jumped out and joined the riot. We made it to the BMW and stepped over the doors.

George was trying to dig the car keys out of a wet pocket. He was squirming around, the cops were winning the battle, the crowd backing up our way, when George pulled out the keys and started the car. A cop heard the car start and apparently thought we were planning to ram his barricade. He waved a menacing nightstick at us and gestured down the lane, so George pulled out and drove away.

Chapter Three

The beach house was another business expense, theoretically used to entertain clients. We sat on the back steps, watching breakers roll up the beach and threaten the edge of our lawn. Most of the steps are shaded by palm trees, and an orange bougainvilla covers the porch, but we were sitting in the sunlit spots, shivering even though the temperature was eighty-four degrees. Convertibles are not great when your clothes are sopping.

"You know," George said, "we don't go swimming often enough anymore." He had taken his loafers off, dumped the water out and set them upside down on the deck. Now he was struggling to pull off a wet sock. George had a good point, but I didn't think this was the time for it. For the first few years after he had enticed me out of the Washington State woods with promises of perpetual sunshine in Hawaii we had been on the beach, swimming or surfing almost daily. After a while we settled into a routine and, except for the constant breathtaking views, might as well be living in Omaha.

George really did miss swimming because for his first eighteen years he had swum in the ocean every day. I would say, "from the time he was in diapers," but George never wore diapers. Hawaiian *keikis* in that time and place frolicked in the ocean and on the beaches au naturel until they were old enough to dress themselves.

"You planning to tell Sally that you just blew up her yacht?" I asked. I already had my socks off. My feet looked shockingly white and wrinkled, and I was trying to unstick the shirt from my back. I tried slapping my head to get the bubbles out of my ears. I hadn't been hearing quite right since the explosion.

George pulled the second sock off, stretching it about eighteen inches long. Silver water droplets glistened in the hairs on his toes. "I

Chapter Three

was thinking in terms of telling her that I defused a bomb that was meant for her." He stood up, leaving a wet print of his posterior on the gray, non-skid painted boards.

"That explosion you set off is not what is usually meant by 'defusing.' Sally would have been okay; Hiro would have opened the door for her, absorbed the explosion, and probably never noticed. Besides, he's smart enough not to go stomping on trip wires. Did you offer me a tequila sunrise?"

"Help yourself. I'll be in the shower. They need to change the water in that marina." George was sniffing himself and stomped into the house, leaving wet footprints and letting the screen door bang.

The beach house has two bedrooms, but only one bath. The sound of a waterfall was coming from the bath, so I stayed wet and padded barefoot into the kitchen. The half bottle of tequila was on the counter. I grabbed ice cubes and orange juice from the refrigerator, but didn't see any grenadine anywhere. A bright red fluff of nightgown that was grenadine colored was draped over the back of a chair, which evoked interesting speculation about breakfast. I was still dripping, so I carried my drink back outside to stand in the sunshine while I waited for George to finish his ablutions.

Fortunately, I keep spare clothes and a few emergency supplies in the second bedroom so I didn't have to borrow one of the atrocities that George wears. We met back on the porch, freshly showered, dressed in dry clothes, and sipping tequila. Since we were no longer shivering, we sat in the semishade of palm fronds that made dancing prison stripes on our shoulders.

I raised my glass, toast fashion, but not congratulatory. "Well, I guess there's not much point in checking the yacht again. You destroyed whatever fingerprints and business cards were lying around."

George took a long sip but didn't seem to enjoy it. The truth is that tequila isn't much of a morning drink, in spite of the sobriquet tequila sunrise, but it was a ritual we were observing, reassuring ourselves that we were still alive and still able to drink.

"We did learn a few things anyway." George's brow was wrinkled to half-mast but this time he was thinking about our dilemma. "At least we know that the assassin came from Korea."

"We do?" I got up and wandered across the grass to inspect a red hibiscus that had just opened. The bush was nestled against the base of a coconut palm like a kid clinging to mother's skirt. It made a distraction and I didn't want to sound incredulous. I don't know how

George knows these things, but he does. My problem was to keep him talking without appearing too stupid myself.

"Well, yeah." George joined me at the hibiscus bush, then looked up at several ripe coconuts that were waiting to fall on us. "You recognized that detonator, of course. That's why we're still alive."

I hadn't, but I nodded sagely and George continued to enlighten me anyway. "It was the South Korean army version of an electrical detonator. It uses a small battery that's easy to carry, and when it's tripped, it charges a capacitor to build up the voltage before it arcs. Takes about half a second, thank heaven."

George wisely stepped back, apparently concluding that a coconut was ready to fall, but not warning me. I stepped back anyhow. I've never seen a coconut fall, but they do appear on the lawn now and then so they must fall sometime. I continued to wander toward the roar and hiss of waves on the beach.

"Did you recognize the explosive?" I asked. "Slower than C-4, but it was a one syllable blast—not two, like dynamite." I was trying to be noncommittal, hoping he'd elucidate without the necessity of admitting my ignorance.

"Oh sure," George said. "I was already running away as soon as I smelled the propane, even before my foot caught on the wire."

The edge of the lawn was eroding in little scallops. The black topsoil that had cost us two thousand dollars to haul and spread was escaping out to sea while the sand marched steadily toward the house. Oceanfront does have its drawbacks, but it's worth it. Watching the waves roll in and race up the sand in a white froth and a seltzer-water hiss is endlessly fascinating. I can well believe the theory that we all sprang from the sea in the geologic past and haven't lost our attraction to the nurturing primordial slime.

Maybe that's why the beach is the right place to bring a girlfriend; it brings out the primal instincts. I jerked my thoughts back to more immediate concerns.

"We'd better retrieve the Jag before the cops notice that it's parked next to the scene of your crime. It's registered in the company name."

Dry clothes made the ride back to town comfortable and really rather nice. I can understand the appeal of convertibles: sunshine on your shoulders and cool fresh breeze in your hair. Maybe songwriters drive convertibles. We burst out from under the canopy of shower trees on Kalanianaole Highway, raced up the concrete ramp onto the freeway and immediately took the exit to Kapiolani Boulevard.

Chapter Three

George expertly wound us through Waikiki, rarely letting the traffic distract him from the shorts and halters on the sidewalks, and dropped me at the entrance to the marina. I wanted to approach the car on foot, as though I had just come from a yacht, rather than pointing out that I was an interloper arriving by car.

A young cop had parked his Cushman three-wheeler police vehicle next to the fence and was rolling up the Police Line tape, no doubt preparatory to moving it to the scene of the next crime. Apparently the police had also concluded that there was no more evidence to investigate aboard the yacht. I wandered over to watch him, tourist fashion.

"Terrorists in Paradise?" I asked.

"Nah, this was an accident. Looks like the pilot light on the propane stove went out. Cabin filled up with propane and something ignited it." Having fulfilled his civic duty of fending me off, he turned back to his tape rolling.

Apparently the "something that ignited it" was either blown to flinders or was sinking into the mud at the bottom of the canal. In any case the cops weren't looking for perps, so it was okay to get in the Jag and drive it back to the office.

The young tape roller had no idea that the yacht was the scene of a three-day-old murder.

Maggie's eyes flicked up when I walked into her lair, but she recognized and dismissed me fast enough that I didn't interrupt her reading. Maggie is more striking than attractive, short black hair, distinctive features that I might take for Jewish if her last name weren't Capriccio, but she exudes an aura of business when clients come in who don't know her. She has even on occasion dropped her book into her lap when she deemed someone worthy of impressing.

Her employment application claimed that she's a twenty-three-year-old Scorpio. I believe the Scorpio part, but I suspect she added five years to her age, and her previous employer history was so phony that we didn't bother checking it. Apparently she had picked businesses out of the phone book. She listed one that had moved to the mainland years ago, leaving only a phone number here, and another that George and I knew very well. Old Smithen will hire a secretary on the day that the Ala Wai Canal freezes over.

Thing was that her application showed a certain creativity and imagination that might be valuable. Then too, George and I don't always limit ourselves to a strictly literal interpretation of all facts. She keeps the office open during business hours, rarely loses messages, and she smells nice when you walk past her desk.

George was on the phone. I figured out after two sentences that he was talking to Sally.

"We'll be up this afternoon to deliver a report. Don't worry, things are under control." He hung up the phone.

"You want to go up and report that her yacht is destroyed and we don't have a clue?" I asked. I reached over to grab my .32 caliber Beretta automatic out of the desk drawer. Maybe I was having a premonition, but we were dealing with a cold-blooded killer out there somewhere. If he was stalking Sally and we were going to meet her it might be a good time to be packing iron.

Chapter 4

We took the Jag; you don't want to appear frivolous or too prosperous when you visit a client, but it was still a convertible sort of day. We get a lot of those in Hawaii, and I guess that's the point. Afternoon rush hour was yet to come, so we took the freeway east to Koko Head Avenue, then wound through the Bohemian atmosphere of Kaimuki and headed straight up Wilhemina Rise.

I do mean straight up. The Rise follows the spine of the hill while Sierra Drive winds back and forth across the hill like a snake, so the first seven intersections are the corner of Wilhemina Rise and Sierra Drive. You climb two thousand feet in little over a mile with a stop sign at every block. When Wilhemina Rise ended in a final encounter, we swung right and continued up Sierra Drive. From there you can look down on the high-rent Kahala District with its walled estates on the beach. The Waialai golf course is on the left and you're seeing the inside of Diamond Head Crater with its National Guard camp on the right.

George had the view, I was looking for the driveway to *Chambers' Chambers* on the uphill side. When it came, the drive was two lanes wide, white cobblestones between cement pillars that supported carriage lights, as well as the cutesy, black-script-on-white-marble, sign. We went straight up another fifty feet before the driveway leveled into a circular parking apron in front of a white aluminum-sided, three-car garage. The garage was connected to a matching white house on the right, and a pedestrian door into a connecting hallway stood between them. We must have tripped an alarm when we entered the drive, because Hirosha was standing in the pedestrian door, his right hand ominously inside his jacket.

He watched us climb out of the car, but did not smile, and closed the door without offering a challenge, but I felt as if I'd just been strip-searched. The parking circle was hedged by six-foot-tall hibiscus bushes with saucer-sized orange and scarlet blossoms. The appropriate route seemed to be a six-foot-wide stone walk through the hedge on the right, uphill, house-side.

The walk led through the hedge, across a half acre of pool-table lawn under tiger-striped plumeria trees that smelled like face powder, to stone steps onto a stone porch, and a doublewide glass front door. We were looking around for a doorbell when the door opened.

The maid was five-foot two, one hundred pounds of picture-book Filipina with the pert figure, baby-smooth skin and large dark eyes that make the Philippines such a popular R & R destination. She wore a plain, just-above-the-knee, dark blue dress, a white lace apron, matching cap, and white tennis shoes like nurses wear. She gave us a little head-bob bow and gestured us into the hallway.

Normally, when you step into a house in Hawaii, you slip off your shoes, but it didn't appear to be time yet. The hallway was like an extension of the walk, only under a sixteen-foot open-beam ceiling. The right-hand wall was glass onto the lawn, the left-hand wall glass into dark rooms. I felt lasers piercing my back and looked over my shoulder. There was Hiro, standing at the end of the hall, not really menacing, but I did not think it would be a good time to pull the pistol out of my pocket.

We passed the end of the house, still in the hallway, and the left side became a dazzling-white stone patio, swimming pool in the center, iron railing around the edge, and nothing beyond the railing. The maid stopped at open sliding glass doors, gestured us out onto the patio, and disappeared. I realized that no one had said a word since we arrived.

A grouping of white rattan lawn furniture; table and four chairs, clustered just outside the door. The pool was kidney shaped, big enough to swim in, and so clear that I could see a quarter someone had dropped in the eight-foot end. We walked on white cobblestones past the end of the pool and leaned on the railing, looking straight down five hundred feet onto rooftops.

"Nice place," George said. I wasn't sure if he meant the house or the location. Waikiki hotels spiked up on our left with the Honolulu business district beyond, the Waianae Mountains for a backdrop, and ocean from Pearl Harbor to Diamond Head making the horizon. Our office building over in Honolulu looked like a piece from a Monopoly game.

Chapter Four

I hadn't realized I was nervous until I heard footsteps behind us and spun around, automatically reaching for the Beretta in my back pocket. It was the maid again, this time carrying a tray.

"Would you care for iced tea, gentlemen? Mrs. Chambers will join you shortly." She set a pitcher of amber liquid with ice cubes, glasses, spoons, napkins, a saucer of lemon slices, and a sugar bowl on the table and floated back down the hall.

We walked past the pool toward the table with a view through the glass hallway, across more lawn to an eight-foot knoll with a curtain of bamboo and banana trees. That domesticated chunk of jungle looked solid so I felt silly for being nervous, and forgot it anyway when Sally came down the hall.

She was wearing a black jumpsuit made of some shiny feminine fabric; maybe it was hostess pajamas. Sometimes you see ninjas on the streets wearing a similar outfit, but not nearly so interesting. Sally wasn't wearing makeup, and that made her more attractive than ever with a kind of intimate frankness. I wonder if makeup is actually a defense to keep people out.

Her eyes were more blue without the mascara frames, like gazing into an arctic glacier without the cold. Her hair was brushed and shimmering that gold-tinted platinum shade. She stopped in the doorway, nodded to us but didn't smile, then sat in the chair with her back to the hallway, pointing us to the two chairs on either side of her.

"You have something to report?" she asked. She picked up the pitcher, poured three glasses and dealt them out. She wasn't looking at us, concentrating instead on picking out the perfect lemon slice from the saucer.

George cleared his throat. "You've heard about the explosion on the yacht?" he asked.

"Yes, the police called. I'm glad it's gone."

George lost some of his hangdog expression and reached for the sugar bowl. "It was a booby trap. Someone turned on the propane, snuffed the pilot light, and rigged a detonator to go off when the door was opened, so the threat is real and it's still out there. The reason we visited the yacht, we were trying to figure out why Darren was there, and of course, who met him there. We're sorry to bother you with this, but we do need to know if you have any ideas."

Sally nodded, sampled her tea, squeezed in more lemon. "We had planned to meet on the yacht and spend the evening, thinking of taking her out for a sail if the weather was nice."

"It was you he went there to meet?" George very nearly choked on his tea.

"Well, yes, we were meeting there, but I expected him an hour or so later. I have no idea why he was there ahead of me."

"And you didn't see anyone else, any sign that someone had been there?" I know, the question was too obvious, but I had to ask.

"Oh, I guess you don't know. I'm the one who found the body. Oh, it was too awful."

George and I waited, glasses poised. Sally went into a flat-voiced recital mode, obviously telling a story she had told many times before.

"I came down the stairs, arms full of Chinese take-out cartons. The door was ajar so I shoved it open with my elbow. I needed to set the cartons on the table before I could turn on the light." Sally was starting to crumple, about to lose it. Either she was reliving a trauma, or she was the best actress in the world. The rest came out in a rush.

"I tripped over Darren's feet, fell on top of him. I could see the pool of blood around his head, egg foo yung scattered through it. I started screaming, ran up the stairs, and fainted on the deck."

Sally let out a wail and threw her head down on her arms on the table. The same instant there was a "ching" from the hallway and a "pock" from the back of her chair. The crack of a high-powered rifle came from the bamboo knoll like an echo.

George grabbed Sally's arm, jerked her down on the floor and threw himself on top of her. That left me with the other job of going after the shooter. I dived for the doorway into the hall and jerked the Beretta out of my pocket. Another "ching" spit a chunk of glass out of the window two inches in front of me and I saw the bamboo move.

My Beretta was in my hand, but it's the model 3032 Tomcat. Its main virtue is that it's only five inches long and three inches high, good for carrying in your back pocket. It's a serious weapon, can put all seven .32 caliber slugs in the end of a Coke can at fifty feet, but it's not the sort of gun you blast through plate glass with.

I was jumping around like I had St. Vitus dance, trying not to make a target. The door by the porch was fifty feet down the hall to my right. I saw the bamboo twitch and dropped to the floor, which earned me a shower of glass on my back, but the window went all the way down so there was no cover. A door at the end of the hall was fifteen feet to my left. I lunged for that, hit it on the second bound. The door popped open and I fell four feet down a wooden stairway.

Chapter Four

I rolled like a paratrooper landing in the wind, not clever, just lucky, and came up with a grass-covered bank between me and the bamboo. I scrabbled ten yards along the bank and followed the Beretta up over the edge. No movement, and from the new perspective, I couldn't tell where the shooter had been. The bellow of an enraged bull erupted from the driveway and Hiro came charging through the hedge. He was blasting away at the bamboo, and I realized that I was hearing the authoritative explosions from a .357 magnum, not a .38. The pistol had just looked smaller next to Hiro.

The bamboo was twitching, and I had it covered, ready to shoot, but the twitching going on was from Hiro's bullets. He fired all six, but kept right on charging, apparently planning to bulldoze down the grove, bullets or no. He made it over halfway to the bamboo, but the twitching had stopped. A motorcycle roared to life from the road below and screeched away down the hill.

Hiro slid to a stop, threw his gun down on the grass and stomped on it. That seemed to use up his steam. He picked up the gun, pulled three feet of white handkerchief out of his back pocket, and wiped the weapon. He spun around and stalked back toward the garage, reloading as he went.

I turned around to see George pull Sally up and hustle her down the hallway to the first room, keeping himself between her and the window. I crossed the lawn and shoved my way into the bamboo, like spreading the bars on a flimsy prison. Branches were broken and grass mashed down, but I wasn't drawing any conclusions from them. Fenimore Cooper's *Deerslayer* I'm not.

There may have been shell casings dropped, but I couldn't see the ground through the grass and weeds. Even my own legs disappeared below the knees, so if there was something to be found, it would take a metal detector, and probably wouldn't do any good anyway. I went back to the house and made a dignified upright trip through the hall doorway. Six bullet holes were sprinkled around the glass, probably a good thing I wasn't even aware of the last two or three.

George and Sally were in the first room, sitting on couches, but not together. Apparently their ordeal on the cobblestones hadn't sparked any magic.

"You let him get away?" George asked, clearly conveying that he would have caught the culprit.

"Motorcycle hidden in the bamboo. He's in a book depository or a theater by now. You guys okay?"

"Yeah, but we've got to get Sally off the island." George got up to pace, so I sat down.

Sally was shaking her head, but actually seemed in good shape for a gal who had just been shot at. "I can't leave the island. In the first place, I'm under police orders not to, and in the second place, I've got a business to run."

"And in the third place," I said, "it wouldn't do any good. If our theory about a Korean connection is correct, they've already crossed one ocean so another wouldn't stop them." Admittedly, our Korean theory wasn't much, but it did sound as if we might have accomplished something.

"Look, kids," I said, "I've got an idea that is so flaky I'm ashamed to tell you, but it just might work. Sally, can you come up with two wigs, a long blonde and a short brunette?"

The look she gave me sure wasn't admiration, but it wasn't disdain either. "Sure, I've got wigs. A girl can't fix her hair everyday." She was sitting with her elbows on her knees, hands clasped in front, slouched over. She went back to staring at the Indian carpet.

"When you need to get away for a while, where do you go?" I got up to pace, so George sat down on the couch again.

"We have a time-share at the Maui Marriott, but I told you, I'm not leaving the island."

"Right," I said, "you're staying on the island, but call the time-share and tell them to expect you. Pack a small suitcase for a few days, put it inside a larger suitcase along with the wigs, and come to our office in the morning."

Chapter 5

Maggie was clearly irritated that I had interrupted her reading. "Sure," she said, "I've been to Maui lots of times, top of Haleakala, road to Hana, Lahaina Galleries, Kihei Beach. Had to fight for my virtue all the way back every time. What's the big deal?"

"The big deal is time-and-a-half until you get back to Oahu and lunch on the company." I was sitting on the edge of her desk, which let me look down on her to emphasize my authority and also prevented her from picking up her book again.

"Oh goody, a company lunch. I've seen you and George scarfing down hotdogs in the Fort Street Mall."

The door opened and Sally strode in, dress dark and demure, but professionally applied make up again. Hiro followed, holding the door with one hand and carrying a gigantic suitcase in the other. He checked the hall behind them, closed the door, and plunked the suitcase on Maggie's desk.

"Mrs. Chambers," I said, "this is Maggie Capriccio, the girl who has volunteered to save the day. Why don't the two of you go down to the ladies' room and see what you can do about switching identities?"

"Hi, Maggie; call me Sally. This is really brave of you."

The word *brave* shot Maggie's eyebrows up, but Sally had bent to gather things out of the big suitcase. Hiro lifted the small one out and set it beside the door. Sally strode down the hall with an armload of clothes, two wigs perched on top of the pile. Maggie gave me a *this-is-all-your-fault* scowl and followed Sally.

When they came out, the hair was switched and they might have passed for each other at two hundred yards in the dark. I noticed Maggie's profile, definitely lacking something.

"Maggie, maybe you should go back and stuff a couple of rolls of toilet paper in your bra."

"Can't," Maggie explained, "it's a training bra and it's chock-full." Little touch of pride there in the *full* part.

"Well, you need to do something, in the interest of impersonating Mrs. Chambers."

"Damn it." Maggie stamped her foot. "It's not fair. Mother and three sisters could do fine in a contest with Jersey cows and I get the figure of Peter Pan."

Sally held up a hand to indicate that things were under control. She bent to the small suitcase and came up with a black lace contraption that appeared to have two fanny packs attached. She caught Maggie's hand and dragged her back to the ladies' room. When they emerged, Maggie had not only gained five pounds in front, but seemed to be taller, head high, almost a swagger. I nodded approval, trying not to stare at the two rolls of toilet paper.

"So, here's the plan, Maggie. Hiro takes you to the airport in the limo. You fly first class to Maui, a limo will meet you and take you to the Marriott Resort on Ka'anapali Beach. You check in as Mrs. Chambers, go directly to the room. Leave the suitcase, the blonde wig, and the toilet paper in the room, stroll back out as Maggie Capriccio, and grab a cab back to the airport. George will meet the seven o'clock flight and drive you home. Oh, and the lunch." I pulled out the bottom drawer of Maggie's desk and extracted the metal petty cash drawer. It held three twenties and some ones, I handed those over.

"And you'll need a credit card to check in." Sally pulled an American Express Blue card out of her wallet and handed it to Maggie. "Sign it like this," she said, making a couple of swirls and a row of push-pulls on Maggie's blotter. Maggie took the pen and copied the signature perfectly. That talent would come in handy if we ever needed a forger.

Maggie, head so high she might have drowned in the rain, walked with such an exaggerated hip swagger that she barely made it out the door. I might have given that impertinent fanny the whack it deserved, but Hiro had picked up the big suitcase and followed her out.

George came racing in, hair mussed and shave sloppy. He looked a little dazed, or maybe perplexed.

"Morning, George, nice you could join us. You just missed the show."

"Oh no, I didn't. I met Maggie at the elevator and she almost broke her neck snubbing me. Something different about her, but I can't put my finger on it."

"Best you don't try. You're picking her up at Aloha Airlines this evening. Better meet the last two flights. Think you can handle the office by yourself for a while?"

Chapter Five

"I'll give it a try. Did Maggie make coffee?"

"Beneath her dignity; make it yourself. Sally and I have to run."

George registered that the demure brunette standing by the door was Sally and did a credible vaudeville double take. He mumbled something like "good morning" and stumbled into our office. I picked up the small suitcase and led Sally down to the parking garage.

"Do you really think the killer will follow her to Maui?" Sally wondered.

"Probably not on the same flight, but if he's as sophisticated as I think he is, he'll figure out her destination and know she checked in. He can spend the next couple of weeks staking out an empty hotel room."

"Are you sure Maggie's not in danger?" Sally's frown looked like genuine concern. I think that's the first time I noticed that she was a human being, not just a rich client.

"I'm sure she's safe. Even if the killer is on the plane with her, he won't shoot in the airports or the limo. By the time he gets set up in Maui, Maggie will be back here. When you have to call the dealerships, remember that you're calling from Maui and don't give anyone a number to call you back." She nodded, I held the door, Sally slipped into the Jag, adjusting skirt. I stashed the suitcase in the back seat and drove us to the Hilton Hawaiian Village at the edge of Waikiki.

We checked into the Tapa Tower as Mr. and Mrs. Richard Payne. A bellman ripped Sally's suitcase out of my hand, grabbed the key from the receptionist, and stood there smiling expectantly. I handed him two dollars. We might need him and the receptionist for witnesses.

"I'll require a computer and a separate phone line. Got to keep an eye on the market."

The receptionist dipped her head, just short of a bow. "No problem, sir, all of our suites are equipped with fiber. We'll have a computer installed in fifteen minutes."

I nodded my thanks to the receptionist, trying to look like a bigtime day trader.

"You go on up, sweetheart," I said to Sally. "I'll be just a few minutes."

"Please hurry," she said, "I just hate it when business is more important than I am." She gave me a smile that I wish she had meant. She leaned over and for a second I thought she was going to kiss me, but she bussed my cheek Hawaiian-style and turned to follow the bellman. Hawaiians do a lot of hugging and kissing. You see the kiss coming, but you rarely feel it. I shuffled back to the car without noticing the sunshine or the flowers and drove back to the office.

Chapter 6

I was having a good evening. My eighty-year-old neighbor, Maude, had invited me next door to her apartment for piroshki and wine. Maude had been mothering me steadily since Betty left, and the truth is that I think Maude missed Betty as much as I did. Betty had roomed with Maude from the day she landed on the island; handy for me, and they were like the best of mother-daughter teams.

Maude had dressed for our dinner date: red cocktail dress, short gray hair carefully permed, and lipstick. We were both in stocking feet, Hawaiian style, but if she had put on shoes I'd bet they'd have been high heels. She was bouncing around, being hostess and waitress at the same time and wearing her happy-but-slightly-bemused smile.

Her sweet little round Irish face must have been a heart stopper in her youth, and if you're the type who thinks beauty ends after the Miss America Pageant, let it go at that. If you can see the beauty in deeply-etched laugh-lines and frank, honest eyes that have met all of life head on, then Maude is a work of art.

"Have some more piroshki, Dick. My, how Betty did love piroshki, but you must try to forget about her and get on with your life."

"Thanks Maude, one more, tops. I'm so stuffed I'll have to crawl home."

"Your appetite does seem to have slipped since Betty left, but let's not talk about her."

My beeper went off, I checked the number, didn't recognize it. "I've got to run home and make a phone call, Maudie, I'll be right back."

"Oh, use my phone dear, it might be Betty calling."

I used Maude's phone and dialed the number on the pager. It was a highly irate George who answered.

"What the blank-blank kind of a wild goose chase did you send me on? I've met the last two Aloha Flights and the Hawaiian flight in between. No Maggie, so what gives?"

Chapter Six

"Just a minute, let me think. I told her to catch the evening flight."

"Is it Betty?" Maude asked. She was trying to hand me my plate and the wine glass, maybe as a bribe to give up the phone.

"No, Maudie, this is definitely not Betty. Be a good girl and pour some more wine, I'll just be a minute."

"Yeah, I thought so," George growled. "You out on a date, me stuck at the airport, and Monica cooling her pretty little heels at the beach house all alone. Hey, you'd better not be calling from the beach house."

"I'm not, I'm at Maude's, now everybody shut up. Obviously something went wrong, maybe an accident. I'll call the Marriott and see if they know anything. Stand by, I'll call you back."

Maude had topped off my wine glass, but was absentmindedly sipping it herself. "I guess that wasn't Betty, huh?"

"No sweetheart, definitely not. Look, the next call will be long distance so I'll nip over and use my phone. I'll be right back."

Maude put on such a woebegone expression that it broke my heart. I wondered if Irish colleens can become Jewish mothers but I ran next door, called long distance information and the desk at the Maui Marriott. That was a bad two minutes. If I had sent Maggie into a trap and got her killed—well, I'd decide between suicide and becoming a monk later.

"Marriott, how may I help you?"

"You have a Mrs. Sally Chambers registered there. I need to speak to her, please."

"Oh, I'm sorry, sir, Mrs. Chambers left instructions not to be disturbed."

"She is there? Is she all right? I mean no accidents or anything?"

"Oh no, sir. In fact, she stopped by the desk, ordered a bottle of Dom Perignon, and specifically said, no phone calls. May I take a message, sir?"

"When will the message be delivered?"

"Her message light will be blinking anytime she notices it, sir."

"Okay, tell that little ... I mean, please ask Mrs. Chambers to call Dick Payne at her earliest convenience, thank you."

"Certainly, sir, have a nice evening."

I called George back. "Guess what, your receptionist just settled in at the Marriott for the evening with a bottle of Dom Perignon and doesn't want to be disturbed."

"Shall I go over and punch her lights out?"

"How you going to get there? You already met the last flight for tonight. Why don't you go warm up Monica's pretty little heels. Just hope that no one else puts Maggie's lights out before morning."

I went back to Maude's and managed to choke down one more piroshki. They really were delicious, but I really was stuffed. Maude poured the last of the Pouilly Fuisse. "It was Betty's favorite, you know." We toasted each other silently, then Maude made a guilty little gesture to the east, toasting Betty, too.

I kissed Maude's cheek, thanked her profusely, wished her a good night, and went home to try sleeping on the couch next to the phone. The couch is two inches too short, so forget comfort, but I did get some sleep. The call came at seven-thirty in the morning, just as I was ready to walk out the door. I'd been debating whether or not to fly to Maui, and the call didn't help.

"Good morning, Dickie, it was sweet of you to call." Speech definitely slurred. I wondered if she had ordered another bottle of wine for breakfast.

"What do you mean, 'Dickie?' What happened to 'Mr. Payne?' You get your tail back here on the next airplane, do you hear me?"

"Oh, don't be such an old grouch, Dickie. The room is rented for two weeks. I may as well enjoy it."

"Maggie, there's a killer loose, trying to kill Mrs. Chambers, and as long as you're there, you're it."

"Oh, don't be silly, there aren't any killers here. This is the Marriott. Listen, Dickie, I've got to run. Kalani is waiting for me by the pool. Ta-ta, as we rich bitches say."

"Maggie!" I was starting to shout, but I was talking to a dead phone. I stomped downstairs and took my frustration out on the Jaguar. The Jag is good that way. You can stomp on it and jerk it around, leave lots of rubber and get satisfying sound effects, and it doesn't mind. I headed it toward the office; I needed to think for a while.

Chapter 7

I knew I was going to have to go get Maggie, but I kept hoping she'd just come home. My problem was that I wasn't sure how to do it. If she didn't want to come, what was I going to do? Kidnap her? If we created a fuss, it would blow the fiction that it was Sally on Maui. If she really put up a fuss, I might be charged with kidnapping, and just might be guilty.

I kept telling myself that surely she couldn't be in the pool with the wig, and certainly not with the toilet paper, so she wouldn't be mistaken for Sally, but I wasn't real sure about that. And what if a sniper thought she was Sally in disguise?

Anyhow, I was putting it off. When I stepped into the office, George had handed me a list of contacts to check. I'd been making phone calls from Maggie's desk—in case a customer walked in—for twenty minutes when I hung up the phone and it rang.

"Good morning, Payne and Clark; this is Richard Payne, may I help you?"

"Good morning, Dick." Long pause. "This is Sally; do you mind if I call you Dick?"

"Oh no, please do, just not 'Dickie.'"

"Dickie?"

"Never mind, inside joke. Is everything all right?"

"Well, there is one little hitch. We forgot about caller ID. Already two people have called me back without my giving them the number."

"Damn, let me think about that. We can set up a call-forwarding service so the calls will come from Maui—fight technology with technology. Sorry, I just didn't think of it. Were any of the calls people we should worry about?"

"No, I'm sure not. They were my private secretary and the

The Dealership

manager of one dealership. Don't feel badly about the caller ID. I didn't think of it either and I use it all the time. Did Maggie get back last night?"

"That's the other hitch; she stayed over, but don't worry, she's fine. I'm on the way to Maui right now. I'll call you from there in a couple of hours."

"Be careful, Dick. You very nearly got shot yesterday."

"No problem, that's my job. Just wait for my call."

I know, that was a macho crack, but what the heck? At least Sally had made up my mind about going to Maui. I took my list into the office and tossed it onto George's desk. He had his phone perched on his shoulder but covered the mouthpiece with his hand and looked up.

I folded my arms and waited so he finished his call, hung up and made a check on his list. Flimsy as the Korean idea was, it was our only one, and a lot of the people on our lists were turning out to be Korean or connected with Korea. Chambers did a lot of business with the Hyundai Securities Company in Seoul, and three of their dealerships carried Daewoo. We were coming up with a list of a hundred or so, which was a heck of a lot better than nine hundred.

"I'm going to nip over to Maui. Home and hearth are all yours."

"Have a good trip, and don't expect me to pick you up."

"Monica give you a little trouble about last night?"

"Do you happen to have a copy of Shakespeare's *Taming of the Shrew* that I can borrow?"

"Bound to be a copy in my desk. Help yourself."

"Have a good trip."

"Happy hunting."

As usual, the parking garage at the Inter-Island terminal was packed. I did the zigzags, working higher and getting excited each time a space appeared empty until I got close enough to see a compact in it. Three empty spaces on the seventh floor were real, a quarter mile from the elevators in each direction. The seventh floor is the roof so your car is going to sit in the sunshine, or rain, but I was happy to find any spot at all. I aimed for the elevators on the left that would take me down to the Aloha Airline end.

The second floor was packed like the stadium during the Aloha Bowl, serpentine check-in lines full, tour groups trying to hang together, a hundred-yard-long line passing through security, noise level just below a roar. The departure TV screen listed Aloha to Maui at ten and Hawaiian at ten-fifteen. My watch said nine-thirty so I waited

Chapter Seven

impatiently through the security line and ran to the Aloha gate. Passengers had already boarded, but the attendant was still standing at the door. We buy our tickets in coupon books, six tickets to the book. That saves a couple of bucks per ticket and lots of time at the airport. I ripped a flight coupon out of my book, scribbled *Richard Payne* on the passenger line, circled Honolulu on the *from* line, Kahului on the *to* line. She took the coupon and I sprinted down the jetway.

The only difference I've ever noticed between Aloha and Hawaiian airlines is that Aloha flies Boeing 737s, and Hawaiian flies Douglas DC-9s. Once you're inside the airplane, it's hard to tell even that difference. First class was packed solid, but my coupon didn't entitle me to that luxury. Behind the first three rows, passengers were spread out, one or two to the row. None of them looked like assassins, and I didn't see any Uzis sticking out of any hand-carry.

I grabbed a left-hand window seat behind the wing for the view of Oahu and Molokai and we started the twenty-minute trip down the taxi way that precedes the twenty-minute flight. Now that I was on the way, the sense of urgency was setting in. I kept remembering Sally's description of Darren's body, egg foo yung mixed in the pool of blood, and fighting off a similar image of Maggie's body—probably Dom Perignon flowing in the puddle.

We climbed for ten minutes like Edmund Hillary on Everest. Koko Head Crater went by on the tail of Oahu, and Molokai popped out of the ocean. If Maggie was dead, it was her own damned fault for not following instructions, but making a decoy out of her was my idea and that was on my conscience. Flight attendants rushed to serve little plastic cups of pineapple-orange-guava juice during the four minutes of level flight, and immediately began collecting empties while we descended toward Maui.

We hit the usual bumps crossing Maui's waist with ten-thousand-foot Haleakala on the right and the West Maui Mountains on the left. I could see up the west coast as far as Lahaina, and maybe the hotels beyond at the Ka'anapali resort area, but Kahului and the airport are on the east coast, I was going to have to drive all the way back.

A Budget Car Rental shuttle bus was waiting in front of the terminal and in five minutes I was driving a nine-passenger van out of town toward the cane fields. I had asked for a compact car, so they gave me the van for the compact price. Such a deal, but the van might come in handy if I brought Maggie back kicking and screaming, possibly hogtied behind the seats. I ducked into the mall and bought a cell phone from Radio Shack, complete with a Maui phone number and roving privileges. That would solve Sally's caller ID problem.

The drive up the west coast is spectacular, with the West Maui Mountains on the right, beaches and coves on the left, the island of Lanai across the channel, and whale watching sailboats in between, but if you're in a hurry it's a twenty-mile-long no-passing zone. Most of the fifty-car line ahead of me turned at Lahaina and at the intersection the highway opened up from two to four lanes. I raced the tourist-packed sugar cane train up the hill and wound through the Ka'anapali golf course to the cubic-block parking garage between Whaler's Village and the Marriott.

Japanese tourists were lined up to check in at the desk, blocking the lobby. I used half of my Japanese vocabulary on an elderly couple who were shoving six suitcases ahead of them. I said, "*sumimasen*" which is supposed to mean "excuse me." They shouted "*Hai*" and jumped back as if they'd been shot. That's happened before, so I'm not sure if I have the meaning wrong or if the problem is my butchering of the pronunciation. If you're wondering, the other half of my vocabulary is "*ohio goziamus*" (good morning) accompanied by a bow, and that seems to work all right.

The lobby opens up to a ten-acre patio, mostly serpentine swimming pools interspersed with lawn chairs and open-air bars here and there. On the left, the high-rise is the hotel proper; the identical high-rise on the right is the time-share condos. Beyond the pool and the hibiscus hedges you can hear, but not see, the ocean.

I started through the maze, passing kiddie pools, waterfalls, entrances to grottos and acres of bare, sun-tanning flesh spread out on white plastic recliners. The moment I stepped into the sunshine, my hackles rose. I could feel the sniper's scope focused on the back of my head. When I looked toward the hotel, I could feel the scope coming from the condos, and when I looked toward the condos I could feel it coming from the hotel. I marched bravely ahead anyhow, working in the general direction of the ocean.

Recliners were positioned between the shadows of coconut palms, the few in the shade belonging to occupants who had obviously gone to sleep and missed the move. None of the bare flesh I was passing appeared to be Maggie's, but most reclinees had towels draped across their faces so I was looking for secondary clues. Most of the rolls had nipples on them and none looked familiar.

A stone bridge led across an arm of pool. A white, circus-tent-

Chapter Seven

covered bar occupied an island, possibly so the tanners could get drinks during rain squalls. The ocean was getting louder, but still not visible. A hundred lawn chairs fanned out on the final cobblestone landing facing the pool, backs to the ocean-blocking hibiscus hedge. Half of the chairs were occupied, most occupants reclining with faces covered and the rest of them essentially bare. That honey-tinted platinum wig jumped out of the lineup like a spotlight, and I could almost see the crosshairs of a telescopic sight focused on it.

I ran past the pool to Maggie and jerked the wig off, probably just in time, but the head I uncovered was shiny bald and reflecting the sunshine. The owner dropped her towel and sat up, half howl, half scream. I felt like the hopeless dolt that I am. Obviously she was a chemo survivor, her eyebrows painted on with a grease pencil. She was sputtering in outrage; I was sputtering apologies, and would have replaced the wig, but suddenly a volcano erupted from the recliner beside her.

He was sputtering too, in unfriendly English, but the words weren't registering, I was distracted by the six-foot-six pillar of muscles that was unlimbering from that chair, and the coconut-sized fist that was balled up. I backed up, still holding the wig, and my first coherent thought was that I was less than a foot from the edge of the pool.

That fist kept right on coming, all the way from the recliner, in an arc that was going to end on my nose. I ducked and dodged, an old reflex from the boxing team, and probably the only useful thing I learned in college. The fist whistled past my ear, and the pile driver behind it kept right on going into the pool. Better him than me. He was wearing bathing trunks; I wasn't. Water from his splash was raining down on my back. I tossed the wig into the lady's lap, she was still sputtering; I ran. I rounded the first six corners I came to before I looked back, no pursuers.

The condos and the hotel are set at angles with the lobby at the apex. That was my only clue of a route through the jungle until I spotted the waterfall and found a walk around it, back to the lobby. The Japanese were gone. The receptionist looked up expectantly; I did what I should have done in the first place.

"Good morning, would you ring Mrs. Sally Chambers' room, please?"

She smiled the hallmark welcome of a Marriott receptionist, enhanced by the perfect olive complexion, long dark lashes, and luxuriant black tresses of the islands. She studied a list, running her finger down a column. I studied the scarlet hibiscus blossom behind her ear, trying to remember which side meant that she was available.

The smile faded, segued toward a frown. She ran the long slender finger with the pearl-polished nail down another list, stopped at an entry and ratcheted the smile back up to half-brilliance.

"I'm sorry, sir, Mrs. Chambers checked out this morning."

Chapter 8

The stoplight at Lahaina, where the traffic picks up and the highway narrows down, took three minutes while twenty cars pulled ahead of me into the *no-passing* gauntlet. I had plenty of time to dial Sally at the Hilton.

"Hi, Dick, did you find Maggie?"

"How did you know it was me?"

"Caller ID has the 808 area code on it, and you're the only Hawaiian number I didn't recognize."

"Oh, right. I'm calling from your new cell phone, so this will be the number people get even when you call from Honolulu. No, I do not have Maggie with me. She checked out this morning so I probably passed her in the hallway when I left."

"Just a moment, I'll check the Internet for activity on the credit card, that might tell us where she is."

"Good thinking. I was going to ask you to do that." That was a lie, but I hate it when the customers are better detectives than I am. Sally was back on the line in one minute.

"Looks like she might be planning to continue the masquerade. She charged eight hundred dollars for clothes at the boutique."

I winced, but Sally didn't sound upset.

"Oh, hold on a minute, Dick, there's another charge coming in."

Sally was gone for thirty seconds that time. The light changed and we started the slow motion trip down the coast.

"That's funny. She just charged an inter-island coupon book at the airport in Kahului, but I'm sure she had a round-trip ticket when she left."

"I'm not sure of anything, except that I'm headed for Kahului right now and it looks like about an hour to get there. At least thirty tourist cars are ahead of me and they're all rubbernecking the sights. Call you when I get back."

The Dealership

The Budget van dropped me at Security. I made it through the metal detector after two trips back to dump my wallet and then my belt. Sometimes you can walk through those detectors carrying an anvil, other times you can't get through if there is too much iron in your diet. I took the block-long escalator up to the departure area and checked the screen. A Honolulu flight was scheduled in thirty minutes.

Maggie was not in the bar or the restaurant, either as herself or disguised as Sally. There was a platinum blonde in the bar, but I took a close look and left her wig on. Definitely not Maggie or Sally, and she gave me a nasty scowl when I stared too hard. With fifteen minutes left, I went to the gate and did the coupon trick again. That time the plane was packed. I stood forlornly by the gate until all passengers with reservations had entered and the functionaries counted seats. I ended up in the last seat next to the restroom with a steady whiff of the disinfectant, but I did have a good chance to check all the passengers on the way down the aisle, and of course, no Maggie.

Sally answered the house phone on the first ring and agreed to meet me in the bar. For some reason, I was reluctant to suggest going up to the room. Maybe it was because the room was rented in my name that made it seem too intimate. I scooted two stools up to a little round faux-stone table next to a forty-foot-tall pillar where I could watch the elevator. Technically I was in the bar because I was under the roof, but there aren't any walls so the other side of the pillar was on the walkway and a thousand tourists were streaming by in the sunshine, ogling the flowers and milling around the boutiques.

At thirty feet from the bar, I was apparently invisible. The waitress was a pale blonde, but dressed Hawaiian: A bit of flowered cloth wrapped around her, almost meeting in front, and woven grass sandals, proclaimed her royal status. I guessed her young enough to be working her way through college, but with a sophisticated boredom and general air of dissipation suggesting she might be a full professor.

She chewed her gum; I appraised the tourists. The afternoon activities seemed to be mostly divided along gender lines. Patrons in the bar *male*, boutique explorers *female*. The notable exceptions were a couple of females in the bar who were bleary eyed and slumping, and an oldish tycoon-type who escorted a youngish lingerie-model type through the jewelry stores.

When Sally came down I didn't recognize her until she was almost at the table. The dark brunette wig was what I think is called a pageboy, square bangs, sweet, innocent, homey, and I guess more ap-

Chapter Eight

proachable than the natural blonde. She was wearing a gray business suit, white blouse, black string tie, and could have passed for one of the hotel executives, if she'd had a name tag.

The waitress must have had the same thought because she bustled right over. Sally ordered a frozen strawberry daiquiri; I ordered Captain Morgan and Coke. There was an awkward moment while we both wondered whether to kiss cheeks, shake hands, or just nod. I chickened out, opted for the nod, and handed her the telephone.

"Thanks, Dick, I need to make about a hundred calls but I didn't want to use the room phone again. Did you find Maggie?"

"Not yet. I called George from the airport and Maggie hadn't come in. Mind checking on that card once in a while, just in case?"

"Glad to. I can't help worrying about her. After all, if she's in danger, it's because of me."

"Hey, don't worry about Maggie." I lied with my usual alacrity. "She's highly trained to handle any emergency." Not true, of course, but Maggie had said that she fought for her virtue all over Maui and by implication her virtue was still intact. Mostly the lie made me seem less brutal in setting Maggie up as a decoy.

Our drinks came and we attacked them fast. Sally was eager to get to work; I was dreading going back to the office.

"Do you have any clues about the killer?" She was playing with the straw in her daiquiri, not looking at me because she knew I was going to lie to her again.

"We've narrowed down the possibilities considerably. George may have a suspect when I get back to the office. You doing okay here?"

"Oh sure, I'm fine. It's restful in a way. I needed to get out of the house even before that sniper shot up the hallway." Sally finished her drink, but did not make the slurping sound with her straw that I always make. I chugged the last half of the rum; we stood, smiled, and Sally strode toward the elevator. I dawdled my way back to the office, enjoying the flowers and sunshine. It would be criminal to drive down the verdant, florescent Ala Moana Boulevard without wasting a little time.

George was sitting at Maggie's desk but he was too big for it. He looked like an adult visiting a kindergarten.

"Have a nice trip?"

"Tolerable. Catch any killers?"

"Getting closer. Look at it this way, if we concentrate on employees, there are eighty-three of them with close ties to Korea. Eliminate the lot boys and the janitors and the ones over sixty and we're down to twenty-five."

"How did you come up with the sixty figure?"

"Well, I figured that if you've been around for sixty years without getting in trouble, you're probably not going to start now."

"Brilliant, but at fifty-nine you might?"

George gave me the withering look that the crack deserved. "I've started checking bank accounts and addresses. So far no one is much below or above what you would expect—oh by the way, Sally called. Her highness just checked into the Princeville Resort on Kauai."

I ran into our office and grabbed my phone.

"Hi, Dickie, nice of you to call. Do you miss me?"

"Maggie, what in the devil are you doing on Kauai?"

"Well, there was a guy in Maui who was staring at me in a funny way. All the guys stare at me, but this one was looking at my face instead of my bazooms, and it was creepy."

"Bazooms?"

"You know, Dickie, the fabulous new swimsuit I bought with the PFDs in it."

"PFDs?"

"Personal flotation devices, silly, I couldn't possibly drown in that suit."

"Okay, okay, so the guy was creepy. Maggie, you were supposed to leave the room rented as a decoy."

"Oh, I know, Dickie, but it seemed like such a waste, and I have a super spiffy suite here in Princeville."

"I'll just bet you have, six hundred dollars per day?"

"Twelve hundred, but Dickie, I have an ocean view and the mountains down toward Hanalei are marvey-fab."

"Marvey-fab?"

"Oh for goodness sakes, Dickie, don't you speak English at all? They're scrumptious."

"Maggie, there is a cold-blooded killer looking for you. Maybe it was your creepy guy, maybe not, but this guy will shoot you without a second's hesitation. What you have to do is dump that disguise and get back here."

"You know, Dickie, I'm not really in disguise. This is the real me. All those years while I was disguised as Maggie Capriccio, there was a Sally Chambers inside me just aching to bust out. Besides, the killer is never going to find me here so no one has to worry."

"Maggie, if I could find you, the killer can. Look, come home and maybe we can get the insurance to spring for some plastic surgery. Heck, I'll buy the hair dye job myself if that's what you want."

"Well, sure, you found me, Dickie, but you're a detective. That creepy guy is just a killer. Oops, got to run, Harvey's at the door. Ta ta, Dickie." Click.

"Any good news?" George called through the door.

"Maybe, Sally might be safe. Seems the killer is stalking Maggie, and I'm not sure I care very much."

"Oh yeah?" George came to the office door and leaned against the jamb. "If she gets shot in the line of duty, just think what it will do to our insurance rates. You headed for Kauai?"

"Huh-uh, your turn. I'll sit here and theorize the list down. If I cut out all the guys under 39 and over 40 ..." The phone rang.

"Payne and Clark ..."

"Dick, it's Sally. The manager of our Hyundai dealership in Hilo has just been shot."

Chapter 9

Hilo was dripping and it smelled like sulfur. The wind was blowing straight down from Kilauea, mixing the fumes from the volcano with the moisture on the coast and turning the whole mess into a caustic fog reminiscent of tear gas. George and I no doubt looked like a couple of executives coming down the escalator carrying briefcases, but the cases contained socks, underwear, toothbrushes, razors, and a change of aloha shirts.

With no luggage to claim, we brushed past fifty greeters who were waiting to lei friends or customers, past the luggage carousels, down the block to the Budget Car Rental booth to be first in line, and I admit, shivering a little. Hilo was maybe a couple of degrees cooler than Oahu, but the moisture in the air was chilling. Plants seem to like it; the shrubs along the walk were bigger and greener than Oahu's, but I was already wishing we'd brought jackets.

We crossed the street to the car rental booths, and, sure enough, no lines. In fact, no one even seemed to be headed that way. George plunked his briefcase on the counter and reached for his wallet.

"Hi, we need to rent a compact car for a couple of days."

Noelani didn't laugh at us, but I could see she was struggling not to. She's a big woman, not fat, *big*, a descendant of the Alii Nui, the ancient ruling class, with suitably large, but regular and pleasant features, and enough ebony hair to braid ropes. She wore her usual open, innocent expression that leads some people to conclude that Hawaiians are childlike. Don't make that mistake for even one second. I think the slacks and aloha-shirt blouse are uniform, but the orchids in her hair were pure Noelani.

"George, have you been in an isolation booth? This is Merrie Monarch week; there isn't a single car left in the lot, didn't you notice?"

"Huh?" George's mouth dropped open. I suppose we were the

Chapter Nine

only two guys in Hawaii, maybe the whole Pacific Rim, who hadn't thought of it.

Noelani obviously felt badly because she always takes care of us. At times, she's even rented me cars that were reserved for five on my promise to have them back by four, so if she said she didn't have anything available, she really didn't.

"You should try the others, just in case there's been a cancellation."

I looked down the lineup. Attendants were leaning out of their booths to see who the idiots were. The next two, Hertz and Avis, were shaking their heads. The girl in the Dollar booth gave a dismissive wave. Alamo had a "closed" sign on the counter; we were in trouble.

"Expecting anything later?" George hadn't quite grasped the situation yet.

"Oh sure, George, I'll have fifty cars Saturday night, a hundred-fifty Sunday morning. In the meantime you couldn't rent a motorcycle or even a bicycle in Hilo. I'm not sure about skateboards, and you'd better not be planning to spend the night."

George finally got it. He slapped his forehead in lieu of banging his head on the wall. He grabbed his case off the counter and we sprinted back past the greenery toward the rapidly shortening line of taxis.

I expect you know about the Merrie Monarch festival, but just in case: Around 1820 missionaries started arriving in Hawaii, and for the next twenty years they proliferated like a plague, intent on stamping out what they considered to be devil worship, which was anything different from the rituals of their home churches in Massachusetts.

The missionaries did a lot of regressive things, covering up female charms, banning the Hawaiian language, and of course, eradicating the hula hula. For fifty years, the Hawaiian culture quietly moved underground until King David Kalakaua was crowned in 1874. King David wasn't called the Merrie Monarch for nothing. He spent his first year as king on a tour around the world, and generally enjoyed the good life, which included reinstating the hula.

I doubt there is an official transcript of the conversation, but it went something like this:

King David: "Let us revive the ancient art of the hula."

Missionaries in chorus: "If you do, you and all your subjects will go to hell."

King David: "That may be, but before we do, we'll start you guys swimming back to Massachusetts."

The Dealership

By that time, the missionaries were mostly pineapple or sugar barons with no interest in going anywhere, swimming or no, so they managed to tolerate the hula.

The Merrie Monarch festival, dedicated to King Kalakaua, has been held in Hilo every year since 1962, and *halaus* or hula groups, now come from all over the world to compete.

Dance contests run from afternoon until past midnight Thursday, Friday, and Saturday. This was Thursday, and that is why George and I came panting down the sidewalk just in time to grab the last cab in the lineup, and why we already knew there would be no hotel rooms within thirty miles of Hilo.

The taxi driver's certificate said "Oscar" and a six-syllable last name, mostly vowels, obviously Hawaiian. Oscar had been standing outside the ancient Cadillac, watching us over the roof while we did our hundred-yard dash, but keeping an eye on the luggage-dispersing carousel, too. We climbed into the back seat, ready to go, but Oscar was still standing outside.

Six very large, comfortably upholstered Hawaiian ladies, wearing matching blue muumuus with big yellow hibiscus prints, were dragging duffle bags purposefully toward our cab. Oscar bent down, stuck his head inside and said; "You guys don't mind sharing the ride, do you." It was a statement, not a question. He opened the trunk and piled in duffle bags. They didn't fit, so he left the lid open and climbed into the driver's seat. The ladies didn't seem to notice us cowering in our corner. Four of them scrambled into the back seat, one and a half on our laps, the other two squeezed in front and we were off. Oscar hadn't asked anyone where we were going.

From my vantage point, buried under muumuus, I could see a slice of sky and burgeoning jungle past George's pained expression on my left, and a matching wall of jungle on the right behind crowns of luxuriant black braids that were as thick as my wrist. The muumuu on the left covered all of George's lap and half of mine, the next one was half on my lap, half on the seat. I was estimating my load at two hundred pounds. We turned right toward town on the Volcano Highway with a scream from the rear tire rubbing in the wheel well. The next two turns were slower, so quieter, and we ground to a halt. Doors popped open and the cab rose two inches at a time as the muumuus disembarked.

We were parked in front of the Edith Kanaka'ole Stadium, which is a block long by half-a-block wide, sixty-foot-tall wooden Quonset

Chapter Nine

hut. Normally it holds three tennis courts, but at the moment it was draped with "Merrie Monarch" banners, had a thousand people milling around, and booths like a country carnival were set up on the sidewalks. A pair of television trucks dominated the parking lot with enough cables leading into the auditorium to wire a small town. The trucks were painted like circus wagons: "KITV-4, Your 24 Hr. News Source" and had the round ABC logo here and there. Drumming and chanting from a practice session were blasting from the auditorium's open portals, just loud enough to rock the taxi.

Oscar climbed back in stuffing bills in his shirt pocket, turned around and asked, "Where to?"

"Chambers Hyundai dealership," George growled.

"Why didn't you say so?" Oscar eased us out through the crowd and back to the Volcano Highway. We raced back past the airport, past suburbia, past a mall, past car dealerships, past jungle-infested no-man's-land. We left the fog behind. Mauna Loa was rearing her 13,000-foot belly ahead of us, filling the windshield, when we slid into a parking lot that had been bulldozed out of the ubiquitous tangle of jungle.

Oscar pointed at the meter, which said sixteen dollars.

George handed him a ten and some advice: "If you'd like to keep that taxi certificate, you'll take this and be grateful."

Oscar showered us with gravel and disappeared onto the highway. New cars for sale were lined up for a block along the highway, two tiers deep, surrounding a prefabricated white office building. We were standing under a forty-foot-tall sign that read, "Hyundai" and no doubt glowed and flashed at night, but the sign that got our attention was a small cardboard in the window. It read: *Closed*.

Except for the occasional car on the highway, we were the only two people in the universe.

"Of course you have a cell phone in your bag?" George asked.

"No, I was hoping that you had a fold-up motor scooter in yours. Want to walk back to that last service station we passed?"

"Well, we're not going to get a hotel anyway; may as well spend the night walking, unless you'd prefer to hitchhike."

"What, and risk getting picked up by sexual predators? We came to see the scene of the crime, may as well look around. Maybe there's a security guard somewhere."

"This isn't the scene of the crime," George pointed out, "no yellow police tape. They either closed out of respect or they all went to

The Dealership

the festival, and I doubt very much that there's a security guard. No point in it."

"Why? Don't they have criminals in Hilo?" We squeezed between cars and walked toward the dark and obviously locked office. George held his briefcase over his head to facilitate the squeeze. "Sure, plenty of criminals in Hilo, but they're all busy growing *pakalolo*, pot to you, and shooting each other over customers. They don't have time to steal cars."

Six wooden-plank steps led up to a temporary-looking porch, two-by-six boards with half-inch gaps between to let the rain run though. George shook the door handle and it didn't even wiggle. I noticed that he did check for trip wires before he crossed the porch. Windows were bare but it was so dark inside that they might as well have been curtained.

"Maybe the back door is open," I suggested.

The back was just as locked as the front, smaller porch, no windows, but parked next to the back steps was a 1957 Chrysler New Yorker, dusty green, with fins and chrome, and I had to take a nostalgic look at it.

"Ever steal a car?" George asked.

"Huh? Certainly not, but I could figure out how to hot wire the ignition and jump the starter. How about you? Car theft in your checkered past?"

George was walking around the Chrysler, peering in windows. "Not car theft, but I did go to a Catholic high school. It was called 'joyriding.' Won't do any good to jumper the ignition because this baby has a steering wheel lock on it; you have to turn the key." By that time, George had tried all four doors and the trunk, but he kept on walking around the car.

"You see, Dick, if you ever want to become a detective, you have to notice details. Notice, for instance, how the dust is all wiped off that spot on the front bumper with handprints?"

"So?"

"So, they held onto the bumper like this," George demonstrated, "and reached under like this." He was feeling around. "And they hid the keys inside the bumper guard like this." George stood up, dangling a ring of keys from a leather fob. He unlocked the driver's door, climbed in, and reached across to unlock the passenger side.

He played with the six-way electric seat, adjusted the remote-controlled mirrors and started up the car. It roared to life with a satisfy-

Chapter Nine

ing vrooom. I'd forgotten what a deep, macho rumble even the best-muffled straight-eights made.

"Shall we joyride?" George asked.

"Could, if we had some idea of where to go." I tossed my case into the back and noted that the seat was almost big enough to sleep on.

"Well, if he wasn't killed here, let's try his house. If he was on his yacht, it's your turn to open the door."

"And just how do you propose to find his house, even if we knew his name?"

George dropped the Chrysler into gear and eased behind the row of cars toward the highway. "His name is William Chun, lives up in Mountain View on Kukui Street, as I recall." George cleared the final bump and turned right on the highway.

I struggled to keep any hint of admiration out of my voice. "You learned all that from reading the file?"

"He was on my short list, second generation from Korea and fifty-nine years old." George touched the throttle and the Chrysler jumped to eighty miles an hour with that velvet smooth float that's characteristic of cars that weigh six thousand pounds.

Chapter 10

The Volcano Highway was climbing, slowly but steadily. Mauna Loa is so big that you never see it all at once so you don't get the impression of a mountain. In terms of cubic yards, or cubic miles for that matter, it's by far the largest mountain on earth, and if you count the height from where it starts on the seabed, instead of from sea level, it's also the tallest.

We'd been climbing through jungle for quite a while when Kukui Street came up on the right and we made the turn. At first I thought we were driving under trees until I noticed that they were ferns. I swear, these were the same old bracken ferns that grow three feet tall around Seattle, but these guys were fifteen feet tall and almost met over the street.

It was starting to get dark, and not only from the fern cover. The effect was eerie, unfamiliar, like a scene from the movie, *Honey, I Shrunk the Kids*. George pulled out the light switch on the panel, and nothing happened.

"Houston, we have a problem," George said. He worked the switch several times, maybe trying to clean contacts. Nothing.

"We have about ten minutes of daylight left. Shall we spend it trying to fix the lights or trying to find Chun's place?"

For answer George stomped the throttle. "Check the jockey box, maybe there's a flashlight."

I opened the glove compartment and found only one piece of paper. Just enough light came through the side window that I could read the paper when I held it up. It was a work order, only one item: "Rewire lights."

A mailbox flashed by and George stood on the brake. He'd been hitting ninety, so when the tires finished screaming, we had to back up fifty yards. I could just make out the name in the darkness, "W.

Chapter Ten

Chun," and a one-lane gravel drive that led into the jungle. George pulled into the drive and stopped dead. It was totally dark.

"Better get out and guide us," George said.

"What do you mean, guide us? I can't see a thing out there."

"So, just feel the drive with your feet, what's so hard about that? Blind men do it all the time."

"Yeah, but they have canes."

"So, grab yourself a cane, there's a million right beside us."

"Why not just leave the car here and we'll both feel the drive with our feet?"

"Dick, this is a stolen car, remember? You want to leave it sitting next to the road?"

"I thought we were just joyriding."

"Misdemeanor joyriding, felony auto theft, whatever. What I really want to avoid is the two days in jail while they decide what to charge us with. Now will you get out there and lead me off the road?"

Total darkness is rare. You can usually see a glow in the sky from a town, or at least a few stars, but not in Mountain View and not under the trees, or ferns, or whatever we were under. To test the old cliché, I held my hand in front of my face and moved it closer until it touched my nose. I saw nothing but velvet black.

I ran my left hand along the side of the car, right hand fending off bushes, then followed the hood around to the front. George was right, there were two gravel tracks and a grass strip between them. The hood ornament on the car was centered on the grass strip. I held on to the ornament and splayed my feet out to feel the edges of the strip.

"Okay, ahead slow.

"Hey, slower, you're running over me."

"Come on, don't stop." I was getting the hang of it, feeling one side, then the other. "Left a little, ... hey, I said a little, come back, now can you keep it straight? Oops, we're turning right, not that much."

We were moving along pretty well and seemed to have come a long ways when I ran smack into a wooden wall.

"Stop!" I screamed.

George clamped on the binders but I was pinned between the car and something. "Maybe you should back up a couple of inches."

"What's the matter?"

"I'm pinned, and your bumper is about to break my legs."

George backed up with a jerk, I lost hold of the ornament and fell onto the grass. I heard the car door close, George stepped on my

The Dealership

chest in the darkness and fell the other way. We heard a car on the road and scrambled up. The car went by twenty feet behind us, but we caught a glimpse of a wooden gate in the flash of light.

"Are you all right?" George asked.

"I think so. Did you see where the latch is?"

"No, but it's got to be on one end; you take the left."

Both hands extended in front of my face, I started for the gate, but ran into bushes instead. I turned right, felt with my feet, found the gravel and then the boards. I followed the boards left, went off the drive, down into a ditch, back up, and came to a post. I started at the top and felt my way down. It was definitely hinges connecting the gate to the post.

"Hinges on my side," George called. "You must have the latch."

"Nope, hinges here too, let's try the middle." I finger walked back along the gate until I bumped into George, no latch.

"You're pretty sure yours were hinges?" George asked.

"Hey, I know a hinge when I feel one, six-inch strap hinge, I feel them every day. Must be on your side."

"Try pushing on the gate, maybe we can tell where it gives."

We shoved, the gate swung open and our reference was gone. *Standing in limbo* came to mind.

"Which way is the car?" George asked.

"Must be behind us, just feel with your feet. Blind men do it all the time."

"Yeah, but they have canes," George growled. He crunched gravel for a second, then a rustle of bushes, a clunk, an "Ouch, why didn't you tell me that the bumper sticks out farther than the hood?"

The car door closed and the engine started. I felt my way toward the sound. George was right, I whacked my knee on the bumper before I felt the hood.

I figured we'd gone about a mile when the grass strip between the tracks stopped and it was all gravel.

"Hold it, I think we're there."

"Where?" George asked.

"Where we're going to spend the night. I get the back seat."

I'd been asleep for a while when I woke up shivering and heard George scrunching around in the front seat. He started the engine, and seemed to be fumbling with the dashboard. The radio blared, then backed off. It was Paula Akana and Kimo narrating the hula contest, but they were narrating for television, not radio, so it was strange. The drums that followed were a universal language. A moment later, George found the heater and a glorious blast of warm air washed over us. I went back to sleep and dreamed about an endless parade of hula dancers.

Chapter 11

About a thousand birds woke me. I could have slept through the peeps and chirps but when the parrots started squawking, sleep was over. I know there aren't supposed to be parrots in Hawaii. I think they belong in South America, but I wasn't dreaming. Hawaii is like that. Let a couple of pets loose, and pretty soon you have a population. Oahu and Molokai are overrun with mongooses and house cats; the big island has frogs and parrots.

George was still sleeping, mouth wide open but not snoring, and he had an innocent expression I don't usually associate with George. His chest was jammed under the steering wheel and his knees were bent double. I decided not to ask if he had slept well.

I eased the back door open and slipped out. It was cold outside by Hawaiian standards, probably down in the sixties, but the sun was just coming up so we had a good chance of survival. Trees overhead made a solid canopy, mostly ohia, or monkey pod trees, but palms snaked up wherever they could get through. We were parked at the edge of a gravel turnaround thirty feet from the path that led toward the house. A new Cadillac sedan, shimmering black, was parked ten feet ahead of us and next to it, a cute little white Miata. The house itself was ranch style, brown shake siding that disappeared into the jungle on both sides with a verandah, or *lanai* in Hawaiian vernacular, running across the front and disappearing into the jungle along with the house.

I was disappointed not to see any police line tape. I had started up the walk toward the house when the front door jerked open and a double-barreled, twelve-gage shotgun blast shattered the morning. The shot was high, more dangerous to the parrots than to me, but I dived to my left and hit the dirt beside the walk. I was hidden from the door by a purple bougainvillea hedge, but it wasn't bulletproof and I could see through it.

Chapter Eleven

The Chrysler's door opened behind me, George came slithering out to crawl up beside me. The house door was still open, but I couldn't see anyone inside and no shotgun barrels were protruding.

"What the heck did you do?" George demanded.

"Hey, I'm innocent. Do you suppose we have the killer cornered inside?"

"I'm not sure who has who cornered. Do you have your Beretta with you?"

"Of course not, I came by airplane. I barely got through Security with my car key."

George was scowling. "Why do you suppose he hasn't shot us yet?" He raised up for a quick peek over the hedge and ducked down again. "Dick, would you take a look at that doorway and see if you see what I see?"

"What, and get my head blown off?" I risked a quick look. We didn't have much to lose. What I saw were the soles of a pair of shoes in the doorway, toes pointed toward the sky.

"You don't suppose the gun misfired, maybe shot him instead?" George's scowl had escalated to the point that usually accompanied his bouts of thinking.

"Nope." I shook my head. "The buckshot came this way only a little high. Maybe he's playing possum, waiting for you to get up and check."

George seemed to think that over. "If he is, there's no point in running back. We'd be good targets clear across the parking lot. Our best chance is to charge him. We split up, you run left, I'll run right, that way only one of us will get shot. Meet you on the lanai."

George bent double and sprinted to the right, using the walk to get through the hedge. He wasn't being shot at so I ran left, busted through the hedge and wriggled under the railing up onto the lanai. George was on the other side of the open front door, doing a sort of tiger stalk toward it. I imitated his stalk and we converged on the door. The shoe soles weren't moving, still pointing at the sky.

We arrived on opposite sides of the door at the same time. George gave a wave, like an orchestra conductor with a downbeat. We both jumped through the door.

The girl, lying on her back, was what we call a *hapa haole*, half Asian, half European, with the best features of both. She was wearing a bathrobe over pajamas, little pink sponges in dark brown hair, and looked to be about eighteen years old. She was stirring and moaning, not unconscious, but with the breath knocked out of her. When we burst in, she tried to scrabble away, but her right arm wasn't working. I noticed the shotgun on the floor, ten feet down the hall.

"Good morning." George was all smiles, already forgetting the shotgun blast.

"Are you the ones who killed my daddy?" It was a whimper.

"Of course not; we're detectives here to find his killer." George neglected to mention the word *private* that should have gone with *detectives*. "May I help you up?"

"I think the shotgun broke my arm." She was struggling to hold back tears; they were escaping, but she wasn't blubbering.

George knelt, felt her shoulder and her arm. "Nope, nothing broken." He grabbed her right arm and jerked her to her feet. I heard the pop when her shoulder slipped back into place.

She shrieked, then a quizzical frown dawned and she wriggled her shoulder. "Hey, you fixed it."

"My pleasure." George made a little bow. "Is that coffee I smell?"

The girl turned and started down the hall, but paused to shove the shotgun against the wall with her foot. We followed her. The hall ended with archways on both sides. She turned left and we traipsed through a big living room with leather furniture and a stone fireplace. Sliding glass doors led to a combination kitchen-breakfast nook at the back of the house. Gleaming white appliances took up the left end of the room, a big oak dining table sat next to a window, and my attention was glued to that window. The jungle dropped away down a hill, and I was looking thirty miles across the Puna district to a dark line of ocean that made the horizon.

The girl turned left toward a counter, opened a cupboard, made clinking noises, and poured three cups from an electric coffee pot. George and I both stopped at the table and stared at the view. Sun had topped the horizon but was still making orange sunrise streaks. The band of sunlight raced down the hill and spilled out to flood the Puna Valley and glitter diamonds off the ocean.

We dragged ourselves away from the view to accept the big brown coffee mugs the girl was holding out. She sat at the head of the table, so we sat down too, facing the window. George on my left was next to the girl.

"Hi, I'm George. That scruffy character there with the hair in his eyes is Dick."

"I'm Lani." She took a tentative sip of the coffee but apparently it was too hot, and she set the cup on the table.

She was well named. She did have a regal bearing about her, ex-

Chapter Eleven

cept for the bathrobe and the occasional flexing of her shoulder. *Lani* means sky, or high places, and denotes royalty as in Queen Lilioka*lani* or Princess Kapio*lani*. Discounting the sponges in her hair and tear stains on her cheeks, this kid had the clean regular features that are a pleasure to look at. *Delicate* isn't the right word, *dainty* is worse, and *feminine* is a cop-out because we have similar features on men, the un-doctored Michael Jackson, for instance. I tried my coffee. It was too hot, but George was sipping his.

George set his cup down. "We were terribly sorry to hear about your father, Lani. Do you feel up to telling us about it?"

Lani dug a tissue out of her pocket and wiped her gorgeous brown eyes, then composed herself like the queen she was going to become.

"I'd been in Hilo all morning, helping the kids set up for the festival. See, we tape a layer of paper over the hardwood floors and set up about a thousand folding chairs. Daddy was home, working in his office." She gestured toward the living room.

"When I got home, I knew something was wrong because the gate didn't work. It's electric and it's supposed to open with a remote control but it was broken so I had to get out and push the gate open. When I came in, Daddy was sitting in his reclining chair." She gestured toward the living room again.

"I said, 'hi' to him but he didn't answer me." Lani struggled to suppress a wail, jumped up and ran back through the living room. George and I just sat and looked at each other. The sun was moving up fast; morning was over, and it was another glorious Hawaiian day outside.

When Lani came back, she had washed her face and her jaw was set in grim determination. I imagine that French queens wore that expression on their way to the guillotine. She sat down and took a long sip of her coffee.

"I knew Daddy was dead because his head was hanging forward and there was a big splotch of blood on his shirt." She almost lost it again, but pulled herself back and continued. "I called 911 and they said someone would be right out. Then I tried to call Sally because I thought she might come over and sort of take charge, but she wasn't in, so I told her secretary."

George was nodding and oozing sympathy. "Sally couldn't come because she's in danger herself, but she sent us. You do know that her husband, Darren, was killed?"

Lani was nodding too. "Do you think I'm in danger?"

"No, I'm sure not." George reached over and patted her shoulder.

I expected her to draw back, but she leaned into his caress. His instincts are amazing.

"Whatever is going on is business-related. Did your father mention anything unusual lately?"

"No, we never talk about the business. Would it help if you looked through his office?"

We both nodded and put our cups down. I'd been wondering how we were going to con her into that.

Daddy's office was on the other side of the hall at the front of the house, facing the parking lot. He had a large, antique roll-top desk, top permanently rolled with a monitor blocking it, and a keyboard and mouse where the inkwell should have been. Lani ushered us in and excused herself. "I'd better get dressed, I must look awful." She turned toward the back of the house; George and I went to work on the desk.

The drawers were practically empty. A few sheets of stationery proclaiming *Hilo Hyundai* and some envelopes were in the top left, pencils, pens, paper clips, erasers, and Scotch tape in the center. The big drawer on the right held a Zip drive and a package of tapes. No ledgers, no piles of correspondence.

"So, what the heck was he working on?" I asked.

George nudged the mouse and the monitor lit up. About fifty icons filled the screen, floating on white clouds in a blue background. He clicked on Juno. Up came "W. Chun" but no password. George typed in Lani and it opened. He pulled out the drawer with the Zip drive, plugged a cord into the back of the keyboard, stuck a new tape in the drive and started zipping. He copied all of the current mail in ten seconds, then opened the deleted messages file and grabbed that. He was opening more icons and zipping, so I wandered out to the living room to visit the scene of the other crime.

The black leather recliner that had been William Chun's most recent resting place had been wiped clean. It was kicked back one notch, comfortable, not reclining. A glass-topped coffee table sat beside it with the outline of a paper coaster visible in the minute layer of dust. Ten feet in front of the recliner was a matching leather couch and another coffee table. That table had recently held a coaster too. Not that the house was dusty, it was immaculate, but when I looked at the reflection from the window in the glass top there was a round area, coaster sized, with even less dust on it. I checked under the cushions where the killer had obviously been sitting, but he hadn't dropped any calling cards; that only happens in detective novels.

Chapter Eleven

One glass sat on the drainboard by the kitchen sink. I opened the cupboard and found seven identical glasses upside down on shelf paper. Two paper coasters were scrunched up in the garbage can under the sink. The refrigerator had an ice dispenser so I wasn't going to learn anything from the ice trays, but there was a bottle of Glenlivet in the liquor cabinet that had been recently moved, and I guessed two shots were missing.

I heard George and Lani come into the living room so I ended my snooping. Lani had changed to dark slacks and a fuzzy pink sweater. I think the Bible says something about hair being a woman's crowning glory. Lani's was like that, rich chocolate brown cascading down in waves that reminded me of those Clairol TV commercials.

"Are you absolutely sure that you'll be all right?" George had his arm slung companionably across Lani's shoulders.

"I am if you are absolutely sure that the killer won't be back. Mother was in Las Vegas, but I caught her at the Diamond Horseshoe casino and she'll be back on the evening jet. I won't stay here. I'm going back to Hilo to help with the festival until jet time."

George handed her one of our business cards. "That pager number is Dick's. Call it anytime if you need anything at all, or even think there might be a problem. One or both of us will be here on the next plane."

Lani nodded and slipped the card into the pocket on her slacks. We seemed to be leaving, turning toward the hallway. George picked up the shotgun, jacked the spent shells out, dropped them into a wastebasket and carried the weapon back to the gun cabinet in the living room.

"Next time you shoot someone with that, hold it tight against your shoulder and pull just one trigger at a time."

We stepped out onto the lanai, Lani turned to lock the front door, and we walked down to the cars. She stopped by the Miata, then grabbed George and gave him a hug, hesitated for just a moment and gave me a hug, too. She slipped into the Miata, and we followed her down the drive in the Chrysler. She stopped at the gate and I ran to open it while both cars went through. Lani rolled down her window and leaned out.

"How come you guys are driving Daddy's Chrysler?"

I walked up beside her car. "We couldn't get a rental because of Merrie Monarch so we borrowed this from the dealership."

"That's funny, I thought he was having the lights rewired. Thanks for being here, Dick; see you." She gave me a wave and zipped away.

George was driving eighty miles per back toward Hilo, but we weren't catching the Miata; it was long gone.

Chapter 12

Lieutenant Holomanu was a male version of Noelani, same large, open, affable features, thick curly hair, dark pussycat eyes, but sharp and relentless as an IRS auditor. Luckily for us, he was more interested in solving crimes than in protecting his territory. Also luckily for us, we knew him well enough to call him Hal, which can save a lot of breath when you're dealing with Hawaiian names.

His office is on the second floor of an old cement building in downtown Hilo with a view across the street between the palm trees to the harbor. The building had survived two tsunamis and had the high-water marks on the walls to prove it. The blond wooden desk may have gone through a world war or two collecting scratches, but Hal, perched on the edge of the desk, could have just stepped out of an Esquire ad: tan slacks, black oxfords, and a brown aloha shirt that either depicted tree bark or a northwest Indian design.

"So, Keoki, what's your interest in Bill Chun's murder? That daughter of his hire you to keep me on my toes?"

Hal's calling George "Keoki" harked back to George's roots, specifically the taro roots in the Waipio Valley. When the first missionary sat down with a Hawaiian to transcribe the oral language, he listened to the fricative sound the speaker made, and had to decide whether it was Guh, Kuh, or Tuh. It may have actually been none of the above, but the transcriber had to choose. In Hawaii, they chose Kuh and wrote the language with only seven consonants, G and R not among them.

When George's mother—who spoke primarily Hawaiian, and wasn't much concerned with writing—named him, she called him Keoki. Anglicize it, substitute G for K, toss in the R and come up with George. We got off easy. The first transcriber in Tahiti was French, and he heard Tuh, so in Tahiti George is Tiohoti.

Chapter Twelve

I could see that George took the use of his Hawaiian name as the expression of solidarity and reference to old times that it was.

"No, a bit more complicated than that." George was contemplating one of the wooden office chairs but decided to remain standing. "What we need you to do, unless you'd like to give us the name and address of the killer, is run a ballistics test on that bullet."

"Any particular reason? Ballistics tests are usually run when we have a gun to compare bullets with. I assume that you made an unauthorized search of the house. Don't tell me you found a .38 revolver lying around?"

George opted to sit in the rickety chair, after all. I think it was a psychological thing, getting his head lower than Hal's to indicate that we were non-threatening supplicants. I couldn't bring myself to trust the other chair, so I wandered over to the window and studied the spray shooting up when waves hit the breakwater across the harbor. With me out of the picture, Hal wouldn't feel that we were two-gunning him. George had the ball; let him run with it.

"Believe it or not, our search was fully authorized by the daughter, and no we didn't find the .38, but we still need a comparison. We think the same .38 may have been used in a murder in Honolulu."

"And that would be?"

"Darren Chambers, same auto group, business connections to Bill Chun."

Hal got up off the desk and wandered over to stand by me, but he was still addressing George. Hal knew how to play the psychological games, too. Let George try to convince Hal's back.

Hal fished in his shirt pocket for a cigarette, but didn't find one. I think it's been at least three years since he quit smoking.

"And if they were from the same gun, what does that prove?"

"Mostly it makes it more likely that we're dealing with just one assassin. What the police don't know is that there have been two attempted murders, maybe committed by the same guy, maybe by a whole army."

That turned Hal around to face George again. "You're withholding information about attempted murders from the police?"

"Until we can prove them. The first was an explosion on a yacht that the police called an accident. The next was by a sniper with a rifle, but he was shooting mostly at Dick, so no one would care."

"Kind of unusual for a killer to switch M.O.s like that, wouldn't you say?"

69

"Normally, yes, but this guy wasn't a very good bomber, and he was an awful shot with a rifle. The way Dick stood up to make a target, any kid should have been able to shoot him with a BB gun."

George was still using psychology on Hal, inviting him to join George in a laugh at my expense, which would put them on the same side. Hal wasn't laughing.

"Anything else you're withholding from the police?" he asked. He strode back and sat on the edge of his desk again so that he could look down on George.

"Nope. That's all that we know, that's why we need your help." George spread his hands to show that they were absolutely clean, with a subtle hint of supplication.

"Aren't you going to tell me that you made Zip files of everything on Bill's computer?" Hal was shaking his head to indicate our sad lack of cooperation.

"No need," George cranked up an innocent smile. "Someone had been into every file after Bill died and before we got there. I assumed that was you."

Hal broke out a smile of his own and gave us a dismissive wave. "Just checking to see if you've lost your touch. Okay, I'll try to set up the ballistic tests, and you know, *Gentlemen,*" Hal underlined the *gentlemen*, "it wouldn't be a bad thing if Hilo nailed this guy before Honolulu does."

"Absolutely." George got up. The game was over. "We never forget a favor."

We tromped down the concrete steps, made the turn at the landing where the light bulb was missing, and passed the high-water marks, left by tsunamis but outlined in black paint, six steps from the bottom.

"There's a cab by the coffee shop." George pointed. "Let's get the Chrysler returned and see if we can make the five o'clock flight."

"Righto." I scooted down the block to grab the cab while George backed out and waited.

"Follow that car," I told the cabbie. Yeah, corny, but I've always wanted to say that. The cabbie followed George out onto the street, then recognized the line from B-movies. He looked to see if I was serious, big bushy eyebrows ratcheting up halfway to where his hairline used to be. He was the family type, running to paunch, so his gray uniform jacket hung open. None of the lines on his vaguely froggish face indicated that he had ever laughed.

Chapter Twelve

"Is this some kind of a gag?"

"Detective," I said, and flashed my badge at him. His expression kept changing like pictures in a slide show, and he was glancing at me every half block to see if I were sane, his ponytail switching back and forth like a horse warding off flies. We followed George back to the car lot with the cabbie getting more and more nervous as civilization dropped behind. When George pulled around behind the office I said, "Wait here."

"Hey, you owe me seven bucks." So much for the credibility of police.

"Relax," I told him, "We're not through yet. When the perp comes out, I'll arrest him and we'll take him to the airport."

George came trotting around the corner of the office. I reached back to open the rear door for him and he climbed in.

"Step on it," I said. "We need to get this criminal out of town on the five o'clock flight."

The cabbie checked his watch: four-thirty. He threw gravel turning around and burned rubber when we hit the pavement, not so much, I think, to catch the flight as to get rid of both of us. He passed cars on both sides, and ran the red light at the corner to the airport.

"Straight to the departure gate," I hissed. He skidded to a stop in the crosswalk. The meter read fifteen dollars; I handed him a twenty and waved away the change.

"What was that wild ride all about?" George asked.

"Some guys just can't resist playing cops and robbers," I told him.

Passengers were already lined up around the side of the waiting room, First Class and Aloha members on the left, ordinary people on the right. We queued up behind a seriously sunburned tourist couple on the right. They were wearing as few clothes as possible and trying not to let those touch them. All exposed skin glowed a deep mahogany red except for two stark white stripes over the woman's shoulders. They were going to have beautiful, healthy looking tans for six hours until the skin started peeling off.

"Well, we didn't learn a heck of a lot this trip," I ventured.

"Not bad," George corrected me. He patted his pocket. "I have every contact that William had in the last thirty days right here in my pocket. I think we can assume that William knew his killer and let him in, just like Darren did. If we're lucky, the killer e-mailed for an appointment, but even if he didn't, he was someone who travels for the company and that should narrow down the list."

The line started moving and I pulled out my coupon book to fill out the ticket.

"Don't circle destination Honolulu." George said.

"Huh?"

"Look at it this way. One day the guy is in Honolulu, shooting at you. The next day he might have been Maggie's creepy guy on Maui. Next day, he's here shooting William while Maggie settles down. Where do you think he went today?"

"And he found her by?"

"Checking the credit card, just like Sally did. That's probably how he found Maggie on Maui."

"So, you think I should go drag Maggie back?"

"I was thinking that you should join her." We made it through the door out of the waiting room and started up the escalator toward the actual gates. George circled *Honolulu* on his ticket. "It'll take me all day tomorrow to go through these files, and before I do that, I'm going to break into the airline computers. If I can find a name that matches our theoretical itinerary, we'll have him cold."

"And if he used a different name on every flight?"

"Then we're back to square one, but if Maggie spots her creepy guy on Kauai, it might be good if you were handy."

I sighed and circled *Lihue* on the *to* line.

Chapter 13

It was six-thirty when I dragged myself into the Budget Car Rental booth in Lihue. I tossed a visa card to Hortense, but all I saw of her was a curly mop of gray hair and one hand with a different birthstone ring on every finger. She ran the credit card through a slot and tossed it back to me along with the keys to a Grand Prix, but she never took her nose out of her paperback version of *Outlander*. She'll do the paper work either at the end of the chapter or the end of the book.

That was a good thing. If she hadn't been distracted, she'd have given me the twenty-minute soliloquy on her grandchildren.

The car she palmed off on me was the last one at the end of the lot. I found it by the license number on the key ring. It was fire-engine red, just right for a high school date. Kapule Highway leads north around Lihue to the junction with the Kuhio Highway. Kauai is like Maui, airport on one side of the island and everyplace you might want to go on the other side.

I still wasn't carrying a firearm and if I was here to spot creepy guys, it seemed like a good idea to get one. I took the first side road over into downtown Lihue, passed one-and two-story wooden buildings that still showed the effects of the last hurricane with corrugated iron sheets nailed here and there for patches, and found a hardware store open.

Buying a gun in Hawaii takes longer, with more paperwork, than getting a U.S. passport for Fidel Castro. My private detective license proves that I've taken the mandatory safety class, but the proper protocol is to buy the gun, take the information to the police department, wait two weeks while they do a background check, then go back, pick up the gun, and register it within two days. That was not going to fit my schedule.

"Look," the bespectacled clerk said, "we're both reasonable men. I'm not risking my license by cutting any corners on selling, so why don't you just rent a gun for a few days? I can let you have this .357 Patrolman, four hundred dollars for a week."

The Dealership

He had led me out the back door of the store proper into what looked like a warehouse, but there was a glass display case and a cash register back there, in twilight suitable for international intrigue. He fit into the warehouse milieu, a carnival barker making a show of being honest, with his sleeves rolled up to indicate that he was a working man with nothing to hide.

He handed the pistol across the counter. It was a Smith and Wesson with a four-inch barrel, about right for shooting elephants at close range, creepy guys up to fifty yards. It had been seriously used, possibly dipped in the ocean a few times, and the serial number was scratched beyond recognition, but the action was smooth and the hammer click was convincing. I took the gun. He took cash, no paper trails, and didn't ask my name or address. He magnanimously tossed in a box of flat-nosed, copper-clad bullets.

Kuhio Highway led between stands of jungle, past mountains on the left, occasional glimpses of ocean on the right, and the remains of sugarcane fields or ranches. Things named for Prince Kuhio are spread around the islands. Kuhio is the name of the second major street through Waikiki, one block from the ocean, and the name of one of the Waikiki beaches.

The most pervasive name of streets and highways is Kamehameha, the warlord who first conquered all of the islands and united them into a single kingdom. That's further complicated because the first five kings all took the name Kamehameha, the last being Kamehameha the V. Some streets in Honolulu are named Kamehameha IV, or just Kam IV, but mostly they aren't that specific.

Several things in Hawaii are named for Prince Kuhio, and I think with very good reason. Kauai has the better claim, because he was actually born on Kauai, but he lost his parents early and was adopted by his Aunt Kapiolani and his Uncle David Kalakaua. Yep, Kapiolani Boulevard and Kalakaua Avenue.

When Kalakaua became king, his adopted nephew became a prince, but then his story took a turn worthy of a Shakespearean tragedy. The young prince was preparing himself for a life of public service, attending a university in the United States, then an agricultural college in England. He was ready to assume his role in government when the Hawaiian monarchy was overthrown.

Understandably, he joined a small group who declared war on the United States in an effort to restore Queen Lili'uokalani to the throne. He was arrested, charged with sedition, and served a year in

Chapter Thirteen

jail. He probably never hoped to be king because he had an older brother, but he did devote his life to Hawaii. In 1902 he went to Washington, D.C. as a territorial representative and spent the rest of his life there. In 1919 he introduced the first legislation to make Hawaii a state. He was only fifty years old when he had a heart attack and died in Waikiki. His funeral in January 1922 was the last state funeral for royalty, and fifty thousand people lined the streets.

His full name was Jonah Kuhio Kalanianaole Pi'ikoi. I believe that the Kalanianaole Highway that runs around the eastern end of Oahu, and Pi'ikoi, a main street that runs from the ocean to the mountains past the end of the Ala Moana Shopping Center, are also named for the Prince. At least I hope they are.

Street and highway names in Hawaii suffer from the Hawaiian alphabet, which has only 12 letters. They have the usual five vowels, but only seven consonants, which make for some long words and a lot of repetition. If you're using one of the street guides and get one letter wrong at the end of a six-syllable name, you'll end up on the wrong side of the wrong island.

Kauai is nicknamed the *Garden Isle* but I've never figured out why. Mostly it's such rugged mountains and sheer coastlines that you can only get to many places on foot or by helicopter. Hawaii, *The Big Island*, and Maui, *The Valley Isle*, are appropriately nicknamed. Oahu, *The Gathering Place*, can't be argued with. Molokai, *The Friendly Isle*, may be open to debate. I would have called Kauai *The Hiker's Island*, but they didn't ask me.

It was starting to get dark by the time I blasted past Kilauea and Kilauea Falls. That's right, same name as the active volcano on the Big Island. Before it got too dark, I pulled over on a deserted stretch of highway beside what must have been a ranch at some time. A line of fence posts stood at crazy angles, but no wire. I picked a post thirty feet away that had a prominent knot on one side and test fired the pistol. It had considerably more kick than my Beretta, but it put all six bullets in the knot, or the hole where the knot had been after the second shot. I reloaded and tried again to get the pistol comfortable in my front pants pocket.

Sunset behind the mountains in the Hanalei District cannot be described; you have to experience it. The mountains are so sharp, rugged, and improbable that you wouldn't believe me anyway, but if you saw the movie *South Pacific* where that view of Kauai was called "Bali Hai," you have some idea.

Princeville does have an airport, but it's a private strip so the personal

The Dealership

jets parked there are an indication of the affluence of the clientele. Naturally, all you see of Princeville from the highway are the golf courses.

Checking into the Princeville Resort is an experience. Just walking across the polished white marble floors with black inlays toward the reception desk is disorienting. It's like walking across a mirror, everything above reflected below. The reception desk itself is four feet high and twenty feet long, made, I think, out of enough ebony to denude a tropical forest, but it's hard to notice the desk because behind it hangs a twelve-foot-square tapestry depicting nearly naked three-year-olds. Two are pulling a cart, one in the cart is impersonating a Roman emperor, and two more out front are leading the parade with a drum and bugle.

Anywhere else, that tapestry with its stone arches and flowers would have looked overly opulent, but in that lobby it just filled the space between the hanging chandeliers and the tropical foliage. The Princeville Hotel is the sort of place where prices are not discussed because if price matters you don't belong there. I definitely did not belong there, but in this case that was Sally's problem. I held my breath and opted for a first floor garden view.

I felt as scroungy as I no doubt looked, but the staff kept smiling, perhaps assuming I was returning from a safari in darkest Africa and hadn't had time to change clothes. My room on the first floor, described as *Garden View*, only cost three hundred fifty per night. I wouldn't be watching any sunsets over the mountains and the ocean, but if I wanted to get up in time, I could watch a sunrise over the golf course. Anyhow, with the keycard in my hand, I was free to wander around the grounds.

A blond table with six chairs in the middle of my new living room held a fruit basket that looked like one of Carmen Miranda's hats, and I could probably live on that for a week. The four-foot-tall red ginger was real. The bed was the size of our reception office, and when I tossed my briefcase on it, it barely bounced; extra firm, and therefore expensive. The temperature in the room was about right for a walk-in freezer.

I found the thermostat, turned off the air conditioning and opened the drapes, but the windows themselves didn't open. Windows, four-foot-square plate glass, were permanently sealed. I suppose the view was spectacular, the promised tropical garden, and off to the right the mountains. If you just came from Omaha, the view would be a treat.

Next to a sunken tub that could be used for a swimming pool hung a lavatory that appeared to be sculpted out of black marble. I

Chapter Thirteen

rinsed off the travel dust, dried on a towel so white I hated to touch it, ran a comb through my hair, and went out to search for Maggie. Dinner was winding down in the Café Hanalei when I peeked in. Then I had to squeeze past the hostess and just gawk. The room was two stories high, with glass walls overlooking the bay. Sunset was almost gone, just enough light to silhouette those Bali Hai mountains, so the thousand-pound chandeliers that hung halfway down were reflected in the windows and the parquet floors.

I got an impression of fifty diners in evening dress seated around tables for two or four, and an equal number of waiters and sommeliers in tuxedos hovering. Several platinum blondes were scattered through the crowd, most with bare shoulders showing through diamonds, but none that struck me as possible Maggie–Sallys. Coral colored tablecloths matched the mounds of lobster and crab shells that seemed to be on most tables. I got the impression that dinner in that Taj Mahal probably cost more than my car. I eased out of the room backward.

My idea was to very quietly let Maggie know that I was there and alert her to watch for her creepy guy, then fade into the woodwork. I was reckoning without Maggie. I found her in an outside dining area called La Cascata where the tables appeared to be floating around a swimming pool, guarded by columns from a Greek temple.

She was reigning at a table for four with an extra chair squeezed in, the other four chairs occupied by fawning Polynesian Adonises. The moment I stepped out from behind a pillar, Maggie was waving and shouting, "Hi, Dickie, over here." She was almost jumping up and down to be sure that I, and everyone else on Kauai, saw her.

I managed to get to the table without falling into the pool. I was making hold-it-down gestures, but one does not shush a well-lubricated Maggie, and she obviously was well lubricated.

The table contained enough shells—lobster, crab, oyster, abalone, and mussels—to pave a driveway, along with the tattered remains of a pineapple and one platter with the Tbone from an elephant steak stripped bare. More to the point were the two magnums of champagne, one on each side of the table peeking out of their individual, freestanding ice buckets.

Maggie kept the introductions simple. "Dickie, these are my friends," she swept an elegant bare arm dripping with diamond bracelets, which I hoped to heck were not real, around the table. "Friends, Dickie is a bigtime private detective from Honolulu, and sometimes I hire him as my bodyguard. Dickie, have some champagne." She swept the sparkling arm again and a waiter in white coat and impeccable smile was there instantly with another chair and another wineglass.

He shoved the chair in next to Maggie, crowding a male model wearing Elvis sideburns and a white dinner jacket, several inches to the left to make room. That caused a shuffle of chairs scooting around the table, which ended with the thinly disguised James Bond, the Pierce Brosnan one on Maggie's right, almost in her lap.

I squeezed in, accepted the now-full wineglass, and caught myself just in time not to call her Maggie. The thing was that she really wasn't Maggie anymore. Her regal bearing was part of it, if you excuse the effects of the champagne. The wig was gone, but her hair was now the same honey-tinted, platinum-blonde shade as the wig. Her makeup and nails must have been professionally done. The makeup added several years to her age, but in her case that was a good thing.

"Sally," I said, "some urgent business has come up and we have to talk privately. Can we go somewhere immediately?"

"Not a problem, my friends will excuse us. Won't you, friends?" The guys were nodding and standing, draining glasses, and I noticed one slip a pair of silver lobster forks into his pocket. It struck me that not one of them had said a word since my arrival, and also that their willingness to leave meant that Maggie would get the dinner check. Actually, a couple of them had looked ready to bolt the moment Maggie said "detective."

Maggie scooted her chair back a few inches and relaxed into a feline posture, crossing her knees in the process. She wore a simple, elegant dress, mostly white with big designer-purple flowers, held up by what I suppose she would call her bazooms. The bazooms were easily up to the task, and I was surprised to note a hint of nipples on them. The dress would have been modest if it hadn't been slit up both sides almost to her waist. She brushed the tablecloth away to facilitate the knee crossing, and I caught a glimpse of open-toed, gold-colored sandals, toenails painted, or pedicured, to match her fingernails.

The moment she scooted her chair, a small army of white jackets attacked, and in seconds we were sitting at a cleared table, adorned only with a few stains from the food and the glasses. The check appeared in a leather wallet with a gold pen sticking out. Maggie didn't even glance at it, just took the pen, added what I think was a one-hundred-dollar tip to the amount, and signed it with that circle and scrawl that Sally had used. The check disappeared, and magically we were alone, floating on the mirror surface of the swimming pool.

Chapter Thirteen

Maggie leaned forward, elbows and wineglass on the table, and she was stone cold sober. The lubricated show had been an act worthy of an Oscar.

"Dick, thank heaven you got here. That creepy guy from Maui showed up this afternoon."

My mouth must have dropped open because she reached out and patted my arm reassuringly.

"I've been perfectly safe because I kept myself surrounded by guys ever since he got here." She paused for a very ladylike sip of champagne and twirled the stem of her glass between her palms. "You know, Dick, I'm not sure that those guys are my friends at all. Sometimes I think they might be after my money." She leaned back again and studied me over the rim of her glass. "So, what are you going to do about the creepy guy?"

That was a good question. I took a sip of the bubbly, very, very good, with nice tickles behind the nose and an overtone of apples to it, and remembered that I hadn't eaten since a quick hamburger at Leroy's Pancake House in Hilo seven hours earlier. I needed to stall for time and maybe try to think, so I said, "Any chance of getting a hamburger in this establishment?"

Maggie waved her arm again, and a waiter appeared instantly. "May we have a hamburger for Mr. Payne, please?"

"Certainly, madam." He dipped his head in an obsequious little bow, and did his disappearing act.

I'm not sure why I ordered a hamburger in that epicurean epicenter. Reverse snobbery, maybe. I love a lobster floating in melted butter as much as the next guy, and a platter of the Alaska king crab legs that had left their shells on the table would be worth killing for. Maybe it was the shells; even crab and lobsters don't look so good after they've been ravished.

It occurred to me that Maggie's beefcake shield was gone, and it would be awkward if my arrival got her shot. Beyond the pool was nothing but black ocean and blacker mountains. The only danger seemed to be from behind the pillars, the way I had come, but an army of waiters and bus boys milled around back there. I was between Maggie and the pillars, and she was scooted down in her chair so that she was pretty well blocked from that entrance by me. I suppressed a shiver, squared my shoulders, and sat up straighter.

My hamburger arrived on a china plate with silver knife and fork and a fresh napkin. It was surrounded by oversized, extra-golden potato chips and garlic pickles with a whole salad of lettuce, tomatoes, and sliced Maui onions. The waiter set a little tray with silver cups full of sauces, none of which appeared to be plain old catsup, next to the plate. For the record, that was the best hamburger I ever wolfed down.

"Can you describe the guy, other than creepy?" I asked between bites.

"Well, he's awful tall but pretty skinny, black hair sort of bushy, big nose, maybe broken sometime, but mostly you'll know him by his eyes. They look right through you." Maggie shivered, and I got the picture.

"Ma… Sally," I said, "It would be best if you could point him out, and then maybe disappear for a while, take a tour or something?"

"Sure, no problem. Tours leave every morning, helicopters, kayaks, sailboats, all kinds of stuff. Dick, you are carrying your gun, aren't you?"

I only nodded, because my mouth was full of prime ground round, but the new pistol was making a permanent dent in my leg and threatening to rip the pants pocket.

A functionary in white jacket, white shirt, white tie, and black pants, topped off our glasses and removed the ice buckets. I hadn't been able to stuff all of the lettuce and tomatoes, and particularly one slice of that fabulous sweet Maui onion, onto the hamburger, so when the last delicious morsel of hamburger was gone and I had licked my fingers, I shoveled a bit of the last sauce, yellow with seeds in it, maybe related to Béarnaise, onto what was left and ate it like a salad. Another leather wallet appeared and Maggie signed it, again without looking.

"Ready?" I asked. "Let's see if we can get you to your room alive."

"Aw, Dick, don't you want a nightcap? There's a piano bar in the Living Room Lounge, and this singer is marvey-fab."

That time I didn't have to ask, I knew that marvey-fab means scrumptious.

"Not tonight. That would be a perfect place for you to get shot. This place is almost perfect; it's pumpkin time." I stood, Maggie was pouting, but she stood too. The waiter barely made it in time to pull her chair back.

"Walk on my left, one half-step behind. If you see him, say 'that's him' very quietly and step behind me. The gun's in my right-hand pocket, so don't be grabbing my arms or anything."

We marched past the pool, past the phalanx of bowing waiters, past the pillars and into a hallway that I could have driven the Jaguar

Chapter Thirteen

down, except not on that carpet; the car might have high-centered. The first cross hallway was as deserted as the one we'd just traversed. I had a flash of that movie scene from *The Shining* with the kid on the tricycle. A few feet around the corner stood a bank of elevators. One opened instantly when Maggie waved her keycard at it. The elevator car was empty, and so was the hall on Maggie's floor. I guess everyone must have been in the Living Room listening to the marvey-fab singer.

Maggie waved her keycard at the detector, the red light on the door handle blinked green, and we stepped into a palace from a Disney movie. I checked the room out fast, then several rooms, including three different bedrooms. Sliding glass doors led out onto a lanai, potted palms, no lurkers. Privacy walls on both ends of the lanai made it an unlikely approach for an intruder, unless he came by helicopter.

Maggie had stood just inside the door while I made my search. I gestured her into the room with a bow, trying to copy the maitre d' at La Cascata, and reached for the door handle. Maggie grabbed my arm.

"Huh-uh, you're not leaving me here alone."

"Maggie, just put the chain on the door; you'll be safe. I'll phone your room, then knock on your door in the morning. Don't open the door until you're sure it's me. Good night." I reached for the door handle again.

"I'll bet you wouldn't leave if it was Sally asking you to stay."

"Maggie, you are a lovely young lady, emphasis on the 'young,' question mark after 'lady,' but this is a business trip, and I'm probably older than your father. Good night."

For a second I thought Maggie was having a coughing fit, then I realized she was laughing.

"Dickie, there are three bedrooms in here. You get the one on that end, I'll take the one on this end. Don't worry; I don't walk in my sleep. Come on, *Top Gun* is on the pay-per-view, I've got a 48-inch TV, and Tom Cruise is … "

"I know, he's marvey-fab."

Maggie picked up the phone, ordered champagne and buttered popcorn from room service, and disappeared into a bedroom. When she came back, she was wearing pajamas and a robe, which covered her much better than the dress had, and the rolls of toilet paper with the nipples on them were retired for the night.

81

Chapter 14

I'd like to say that it was surf pounding on the rocks that woke me, but it was probably a helicopter full of tourists taking off. The wall of my room was all glass, so I could see the blue dome of sky, with just enough white cotton balls floating to keep it from being boring. With the sun behind me, the mountains across the bay looked too stark to be real, like an over-enhanced television picture.

Surf was pounding on rocks and shooting up spray. Princeville is built where it is for the view, not the beaches, and the beaches look pretty sparse compared to Waikiki—unless you know that most of the sand on Waikiki's beaches was hauled in by truck and spread over lava rock.

By the way, Princeville was not named for Prince Kuhio. It was named many years earlier for Prince Albert, son of King Kamehameha the IV and Queen Emma, back when all of this was a sugarcane and coffee plantation.

A tray on the white-marble top next to the gold-tinted mirror in the bathroom had a toothbrush in a cellophane wrapper. I bit the end off the cellophane, helped myself to toothpaste, and a disposable razor, and ignored several little bottles that I didn't recognize. There's just enough Scotch in me, genes, not liquor, that it bothers me to use a razor once, or three times at home, and throw it away, when all except the tiny double blade is still good; but that is the American way. The disposable razors cost less than replacement blades for real razors.

Maggie was sitting on the couch dressed in a very chic jungle-green pants suit, bazooms in place, drinking coffee from a room service tray and nibbling the remains of last night's popcorn orgy.

"Good morning, Rip Van, I thought you were going to sleep all day."

"Jet lag?" I tried.

"Between here and Oahu?"

Chapter Fourteen

"Hey, I came all the way from Hilo." I helped myself to the coffee. Like everything in Princeville, it wasn't just coffee, it was an experience. Naturally it was Kona Coffee, but there had to be more to it, and I think I detected an aftertaste of vanilla. Anyhow, it was waking me up and I tried a couple of fluff balls of leftover popcorn. The butter that was melted last night was congealed this morning, but otherwise they weren't half bad.

Maggie reached for a room service menu that sat by the telephone.

"Huh-uh," I said. "We need to find your creepy guy, the sooner the better, before he has a chance to scope out your schedule and learn the hotel. Do they serve breakfast in the Café Hanalei?"

We assumed our formation and braved the hallway. I didn't much like that, because there were too many doors. I had my hand on the magnum and had it half pulled out of my pocket, but if a door suddenly opened, either in front or behind us, and someone came out shooting, there wouldn't be much time and no cover. The family in the elevator wore beach robes over bathing suits, except for the toddlers who wore only the suits. I shoved the gun back down in my pocket. Apparently we were invisible anyway, they never even noticed us.

Café Hanalei was bustling with breakfast sounds and smells, populated with aloha shirts, polo shirts, and shorts. We were ushered to a table near the window by a sylphic teenage wahini wearing a beige Tahitian muumuu that wouldn't clash with anything. She wore high-heeled sandals and had very nice legs, which were evident because the muumuu had four slits to the panty line. She also had enough ebony hair that she needn't have worn a top.

She tried to seat us at a table for four on the ocean view side with our backs to the room. She looked scandalized when I walked around the table and sat facing the room. She punished me by removing the silver and glasses from the view side of the table. The waiter, who was poised to pull out the view chair for Maggie, had to dash around, but he recovered in time. Napkins that matched the salmon-colored tablecloth were folded into rooster tails. He ripped Maggie's napkin off the table and spread it in her lap. I managed to slide my own chair and unfold my own napkin.

Beverages appeared instantly: ice water, coffee, and a morning version of a sommelier. He wasn't asking if we wanted juice, he was asking if we wanted orange or pineapple. I opted for the pineapple and checked out the tray of half-sized Danish next to a boat full of whipped butter that had dropped from heaven onto the center of the table. The sunrise som-

The Dealership

melier hovered; Maggie downed half her orange juice in one gulp, so he refilled it. Little legacy of the popcorn, I suppose.

The menu was a leather-bound book reminiscent of a first-edition Dickens. I started through it: fancy script, but pictures so that if you didn't speak English you could just point. I gave up. I think they served everything that has ever been ordered for breakfast. If you hanker to start your day with an emu steak, they probably had it. I ordered eggs Benedict and Maggie ordered a crab omelette, also without looking. I hoped that a restaurant with that much class might not tart up the Benedict with turkey, and would probably have the traditional black olives on top.

I had just taken my first sip of fresh pineapple juice and was eyeing the tray of Danish again, when Maggie grabbed my arm.

"That's him," she hissed. She had gone pale, and may have been thinking of sliding under the table.

I patted her hand and whispered, "Calm down, it's okay."

She had described Spencer to a T, except she hadn't mentioned his badge because he wasn't wearing it. He marched his elegant frame behind the slit muumuu to a table at the back of the room and sat facing the room, but from his table he was also facing the view so he didn't cause a stir.

"Maggie," I said, "Spencer is a senior agent for the DEA in Honolulu. Come on, I'll introduce you." I started to stand, but Spencer met my eyes and gave me an almost imperceptible head shake. That meant he was on a case and did not want to be recognized. It also meant that someone in the room was in a lot of trouble and probably didn't know it yet, but for a change it wasn't us. I lifted the Canadian bacon with my knife, pulled the turkey out from under it with the fork, and dug in. It was better than most, but so far no restaurant has ever used enough lemon juice to make a really good hollandaise. It did have the traditional black olives on top.

Maggie had massacred her crab omelet and sat back with her coffee while I was still soaking up the last of the hollandaise with the edge of the hash browns.

"You know, Dick, all of this has got pretty boring. I think I'd like to get back to work."

I almost choked on the hash browns until she elaborated.

"I was reading a really great book about a beautiful rich girl who meets a handsome detective, and they are going to set sail on his yacht for some tropical paradise." Her eyes clouded over with the same expression George has when he's contemplating things we can't afford.

Chapter Fourteen

A bellman brought Maggie's suitcase to the curb. It was the same big case she left Honolulu with, but considerably heavier. The bellman was trying not to sneer at that bright red Grand Prix and I tipped him five dollars for his effort. Maggie came bouncing down the steps; it had taken her a bit longer to check out.

"Wow, Dick, nice wheels. Too bad you don't have a classy car like this in Honolulu."

We'd made it past Kilauea to that deserted stretch that used to be sugarcane when I noticed a big black station wagon coming up fast behind us. Very, very fast, and I expected him to pass with a *whish*, so when he slowed down beside us, I looked over and stared into the barrel of an automatic weapon. I saw a glimpse of the guy behind it, and he could have been a brother to Cy, the bartender at Fat Fat.

I slammed on the brakes, the wagon shot ahead, and a burst of automatic fire grazed past our windshield. I hissed at Maggie to get down, but she had already dropped her seat belt and was on the floor. I stomped the gas pedal. The wagon had slowed down and was still in the left-hand lane. I slammed the center of our bumper into his right rear, trying to cause a skid. The wagon was too heavy and the driver was too good. He controlled the skid and leapt ahead.

By the time I got the pistol out of my right-hand pocket, got the window down and the pistol sticking out of it in my left hand, the wagon was fifty yards ahead. The Grand Prix topped out at a hundred and five; maybe the rentals have a governor on them. The hurricane outside the window was trying to rip the pistol out of my hand.

That automatic pistol came out the passenger window ahead of us and I saw the muzzle flash, but the wind was whipping it around. I took the left lane to keep the wagon between us and the weapon, braced the .357 against the mirror, and emptied it at the back of the wagon. I was hitting the wagon; he did some swerving and I saw the rear window cloud over where the bullets hit it, but he kept on accelerating. I was going to lose him, and once he was out of sight, he'd be lethal again.

I stomped the brake, forgetting about Maggie, and jammed her clear under the dashboard. When the tires finished howling and sliding, she scrambled into the seat, and by the time I had backed around in a half-circle and headed back the way we had come, she was tightening her belt. The problem was that we were trapped.

There is only one road along the north side of Kauai, or around any side for that matter, and you cannot drive around the island. The northwest end of Kauai, the Na Pali Coast, is so rugged and inaccessible that the only people who have ever seen it were hikers, or in boats or helicopters. The word *pali* means cliff, and that describes the whole coastline. With the station wagon between us and the airport, and especially in that bright red fire engine we were driving, there could be an ambush behind every tree for the next thirty miles.

I expected Maggie to be terrified, but when I glanced over she was unwrapping a stick of gum. I glanced fast because we were hitting ninety; I only slowed down to seventy when we flashed through Kilauea.

"Gee, Dick, this is pretty exciting. Do you get shot at all the time?"

"No, Maggie, I do not make a habit of getting shot at."

"Well, when Sally was stuffing my new bazooms, she mentioned that you ran straight toward a guy who was shooting at you with a rifle. How can you be so brave when you look like such a dork?"

That was a fair question but I let it slide, we were sliding into the parking lot at Princeville, anyhow. The lot had emptied out for the daytime and I found a spot close to where one of the tour helicopters was parked. The pilot was sitting on the grass drinking a can of Coke, but he stood up when he saw us running across the lawn toward the chopper.

He was too tall and too thin, but he moved with an athletic grace. When we got close I saw that he was also too young. His youth was accented by a blond brush cut that used to be called a flat top. Innocent blue eyes, matching blue aloha shirt, and tan slacks with brown loafers, completed the picture of a college kid.

The chopper was an ASTAR, a spin-off of the Bell Jet Ranger, but with more windows, and this one looked like it was camouflaged for jungle fighting: green tail, and banana leaves were painted up and around the fuselage. I had already ripped the back door open and shoved in Maggie and the suitcases when the pilot came trotting up.

"Hey, the next tour isn't for an hour. I'm taking my break."

"We're not taking a tour. You're taking us to the airport, now."

Sometimes the chemistry is just wrong between two people, and maybe I wasn't very diplomatic—I was still coming down from the rush of being shot at. In any case, I got his back up. He crossed his arms, shook his head. I did not like this kid, he obviously did not like me, but this was no time for a therapy session, and I noticed that I wasn't getting any calmer.

"I'm not taking you anywhere." Maybe he was Swedish; his lower lip stuck out in monumental stubbornness.

"Oh yes, you are, you're taking us to the airport, and I said now."

Chapter Fourteen

"You going to make me, Pops?"

"If necessary, certainly. First, I'll try offering you four hundred dollars for a forty-minute flight. If that doesn't work, I'll rip your arms off, beat that smarmy smile off your face with the bloody ends, and fly the bird myself."

He glanced around for reinforcements, but no one was close. Apparently he realized that I was serious, and I wasn't bluffing. I could have flown the bird myself, but that's ancient history and another story. I was wavering, almost tempted to show him the pistol, but not wanting to escalate this squabble into a federal hijacking case. I wasn't interfering with a flight crew; we weren't flying.

"You said, four hundred, cash. No checks, no credit cards?"

I nodded, he walked around and climbed in.

The turbine wound up fast. He picked us straight up three feet, scanned the panel and started his run sideways down the hill toward the water before he straightened out and pulled us into a climbing turn back over the parking lot, headed for the airport. He was a little overanxious on the climb and let the RPMs creep over the red line. I couldn't resist.

"Watch your rotor speed," I snapped. "I want to get to the airport alive." He did a double take and backed off the throttle a hair. He kept climbing, intending to short cut across the low mountains on the north east corner of the island.

"Hold it at five hundred feet, and follow the highway." He shrugged and swerved back over the road. The spot where we'd been ambushed was marked by rubber tracks that looked like those Japanese Sumi paintings. I scanned crossroads and lanes, looking for the station wagon, but too many possibilities were covered by trees and I didn't see it. That was probably good, because the pilot might have had serious objections to making a strafing run. The jet wasn't there, so he parked on the apron right in front of the passenger terminal. We scrambled out.

"Hey, where's my four hundred dollars?"

"Most of it's inside in a cash machine. Come on in with us." He locked down the controls and left the blade spinning. I lugged the suitcase; Maggie lagged behind, eyeing the pilot, eyes glazed over again. Fortunately, there was a Banko ATM in the lobby. It grudgingly gave me three hundred in twenties. I emptied my pockets, came up with sixty-three dollars more, and looked at Maggie. She opened her little purse and saved the day with two more twenties. I took the odd three dollars back—it's not polite to tip pilots. He stalked out, Maggie wavered, barely resisted following, and I headed for the bank of phones.

"Hey, George, he's here. I've got him trapped, only there's two of him now. I'm sending Maggie home on the next plane."

"Good work. Did you use a bear trap or is his hand stuck in the cookie jar?"

"Not quite that simple. He's on the north side of Kauai, I'm at the airport, so he can't get past me, and I'll recognize him. He looks just like Cy at Fat Fat."

"That's good, Dick. You've got him trapped on fifty miles of roads with two or three towns and umpteen resorts. Don't let him get away. Did he tell you that he gets seasick or is otherwise allergic to boats?"

"Okay, okay, so he still requires some flushing out. Are you going to come help me, or sit there yammering all day?"

"Oh, I'll come over and hold your hand, but I think you should know that I've narrowed the field to four hot prospects, and all of them are right here on Oahu right now. Also, it may interest you that Sally has done a bunk."

"She's what?"

"Done a bunk. Mr. and Mrs. Dick Payne checked out of the Tapa Tower this morning. She didn't call and she didn't leave a forwarding address—except of course this one. I talked the hotel clerk into giving me this address off the credit card you used."

"Did you check her house?"

"I was about to, unless you want me to come chase wild geese on Kauai. Bear in mind that the four guys who knew both victims, travel for the company, and might have been in Hilo at the right time, are all here now, none hiding in the bushes on Kauai."

"Okay, so we're up against some kind of organization, and what I have here are a couple of soldiers. It still would be good to go after them. They might answer questions, but maybe you'd better stay there."

"Do you want me to mail your Beretta? It's right here in your desk drawer."

"Never mind, I rented a cannon. Look, a jet is just landing and I'll stick Maggie on it before she changes her mind. You stay after the big fish. I'll just handle the little guys with the submachine guns. You can pick up Maggie in thirty minutes." I hung up the phone and lugged Maggie's suitcase to the check in. She still had most of her book of interisland tickets.

Chapter 15

Since I already had a car rented from Budget, I decided not to muddy the waters. A cute little girl hiding behind granny glasses and pigtails, wearing a sharp aloha-shirt-and-slacks outfit, rented me a car at Avis. When I asked for something inconspicuous and fast she looked me over, but apparently decided I was not a teenage suicide candidate. She probably thought I was just one of the usual Kauai drug runners, and rented me a gray Honda Civic. I don't know about the fast, but you can't get less conspicuous in Hawaii.

I raced back to the junction with Kuhio Highway so there was only one route to the airport, pistol reloaded and on the seat beside me. I figured that the bad guys would set up an ambush and wait for the red car for a while, and when it didn't come, maybe backtrack to look for it. Coming from the wrong direction in the wrong car and without the blonde gave me a good chance of surprising them.

My fantasy involved finding the black station wagon parked on some little lane into the jungle, both guys out leaning across the hood with their rifles pointed back toward Princeville. In that scenario, I shot the rifles out of their hands, they gave up and marched obediently to the nearest police station and spilled their guts. That was the fantasy. The reality was that I drove slowly, checking out every lane and crossroad, all the way back to Princeville. No black station wagon was parked in any of the hundred or so perfect ambush spots I passed.

The parking lot outside the hotel was filling up again, people returning from their tours of the canyons, caves, and the Hanalei beaches. I drove through the crowded lot anyhow, toward the parked red Pontiac, and there sat the station wagon, parked right beside it. I didn't see any gunmen sitting in the wagon, but they could have been scrunched down waiting for us to come back to the Pontiac. I

The Dealership

drove right on past and found a parking spot by the perimeter road a quarter mile away.

One of the nice things about aloha shirts is that they can be worn with the tail out, and if you do that, you can stick a gun, even an oversized .357, in your back pocket, or rather, half in the pocket. You can get it fast, and it doesn't show. I was keeping a sharp lookout, maybe ducking occasionally when I imagined bullets whizzing past, but I didn't see anyone, and worked my way up to the line of cars behind the station wagon.

It was hard to see into the wagon because three bullet holes in the back window made white clouds of the shatter-proofing plastic in the glass around them, but I watched a while anyway. No heads came up to look around. I moved the gun up to stick the barrel in the front pocket, keeping the butt in my hand and at least half hidden by the shirt. No help for it, I had to do a casual stroll past that wagon to get a look down between the seats. I sauntered, unconcerned and uninterested, everything except whistling. Blankets and fast food wrappers were scattered on the floor between the seats, but no gunmen. That made it worse; they were probably hunkered down at the edge of the helicopter pad waiting for me to stroll into their trap. It was too late to duck and run, so I kept strolling, trying to look like the most innocent tourist, but my finger kept trying to tighten around the pistol trigger.

A green camouflaged helicopter came scooting across the bay, slowed down and hovered onto the pad. I stepped back toward the lot until the windstorm abated. Happy tourists with video cameras came tumbling out, and the pilot who rushed to help them was the same one who had taken us to the airport. He had his hand out, collecting, so I was wrong about tipping pilots.

Tourists gathered their paraphernalia and trooped off toward the hotel. The pilot looked up and saw me standing there. His mouth dropped open, his hands went halfway up, and he was backtracking after the tourists, taking backward steps five feet long.

"Hey," I said, "what's your problem? We made you a heck of a good deal."

He slowed a little but wasn't stopping. I had to follow to stay within shouting distance.

"Yeah," he said, "you did, but those two friends of yours sure didn't."

"What friends, what are you babbling about?" He was still walking backward but misjudged his route, ran into a hibiscus bush, and

Chapter Fifteen

had to stop. I stayed far enough away not to be too threatening, and took my hand off the pistol for good measure. "What do you mean, 'friends of mine'?"

"When I got back from the airport, your two buddies were waiting. They stuck guns in my face and demanded a ride to the airport, too."

"And you took them?"

"What would you have done?"

I shoved the pistol down into the pocket and ran for the hotel.

I tried ringing George from a pay phone, no answer. Why the heck was I the one who wore the pager? I tossed the Pontiac keys to an impeccable mannequin who was modeling for a male fashion magazine behind the reception desk.

"These are to a Budget Rent-A-Car parked in the side lot. I'd like to turn it in here."

"Certainly, sir." I suspect those may be the only English words some of the hotel employees know, but this guy had a full command of the language. "There's a fee for dropping it off. It will be on your credit card statement." That was my cue to tip him, but all the cash I had left was the three dollars from the airport transaction. I gave him a thumbs up instead and sprinted back to the Honda.

Twenty passengers were lined up waiting for the next jet, none who looked like Cy. I kept my hand on the pistol anyhow, checked out the parking lot and the restrooms. The only suspicious character I saw was a guy in the restroom taping plastic bags of marijuana to his ankles. He gave me a fishy mind-your-own-business stare, and I did. Some people don't believe pakalolo packing is that obvious, but then, they haven't been to Kauai. I really didn't expect any trouble at the airport because at least two planes had departed for Honolulu while I checked out the empty road to Princeville.

The gunmen wouldn't think I'd be stupid enough to stay on Kauai, so they probably caught the next jet to Honolulu in hot pursuit. The guy with the baggy pants came out of the restroom, so I went in, wiped the fingerprints off the gun, and dumped it into the garbage, along with the box of shells.

I'd look pretty silly, and maybe suspicious, if I checked my briefcase, and unless the metal detector was really on the fritz, I wasn't going to make it onto the airplane carrying that cannon. I heard the next jet pull up outside. It's hard to miss because it shakes the entire building. I ventured out, feeling naked, made it through security, and joined the queue.

Chapter 16

Maggie was seated at her desk and looked up with a bright smile. Hi Di... Mr. Payne. She went back to reading. She was still platinum blonde, but the bazooms had shrunk. I judged the size halfway between Sally and Maggie, very definite nipples on them.

I stopped beside her desk and she looked up, more curious than annoyed at the interruption.

"Maggie," I said, "people who have been shot at together are usually on a first name basis. Call me Dick when there are no customers here, but I can do without 'Dickie.'"

She gave me a smile, and I take back that crack I made about her not being beautiful. When she was lit up by that smile, she was gorgeous, and it wasn't just the blonde hair.

"Thanks, Dick, and you may call me Maggie, no more 'Miss Capriccio' unless we have customers."

I think I had just been scolded for sexism or something like that. I was still pondering that when I stepped into our office.

"Welcome home, Nimrod, where are your prisoners?" George had papers on his desk, but his feet were up and a cup of coffee was steaming beside the papers.

"Tried to escape, so I shot them," I growled. "Did you arrest Mr. Big yet?"

"Soon, very soon. I've narrowed it down to one accountant and one sales rep. I'm just waiting for one of them to make a false move."

"And that false move would be to shoot Sally? Speaking of Sally, did you find her, or is she already shot?"

"Well, she answered her cell phone and said it's best if even we don't know where she is. She may have the idea that we led that sniper up to her house. Do you suppose we did?"

"Possible. You were riding shotgun, so you were supposed to be keeping an eye out for a tail, but actually, I doubt that we're guilty. I think the

Chapter Sixteen

sniper was already there, but it certainly was us who lured Sally out onto the lanai where he could get a shot at her. So, where is she?"

George dragged his feet off the desk and tossed the papers over onto my desk, so I sat down. He got up to check the window in case Honolulu was missing.

"Sally went back to her house, no question about it. When I drove by, Hiro was standing outside on permanent guard duty, and when I phoned the house number and asked for Sally, the maid got so flustered she forgot how to speak English."

"Any idea why she took off?" I asked.

"Phone rang in her room, she forgot and answered it. The caller hung up. Maybe nothing, probably a wrong number, but Sally panicked."

The papers that George had tossed on my desk were his version of dossiers on two of Sally's employees. Harry Kim was a sales rep for Daewoo, Ronald Murphy was in corporate accounting.

"Ronald Murphy is Korean?"

"Yep, born in Pusan, the Irishman in the woodpile was his grandfather."

"How come you settled on these two?"

"Both had appointments with William Chun. I got that off his e-mail."

"For the day of the murder?" I was leafing down through the dossiers, four single-spaced typed pages in each. I had the Kim pile on the left, the Murphy file on the right, turning over a page in each simultaneously.

"No, both appointments were for the following week, but I figure since he was expecting them, he wouldn't have been too surprised if one showed up a few days early, maybe explaining that they happened to be passing."

"Pretty flimsy evidence."

"There's more. Chun's files also got me into the corporate credit card account. Every one of their executives carries an American Express Card, all on the same account. Once you're into the account, type in the name and there's their whole life. The days of Big Brother watching are sure here, if he wants to."

"So, these two guys charged tickets to Hilo?"

"Nope, other way around. Almost everyone on my short list charged something the day of the murder. Several went to dinner at the Honolulu Club, some were on other islands, one got his fortune told by Madam Zenobia. Anyhow, they couldn't have been in Hilo at the right time. I also went back to the day of Darren's murder and eliminated a few more. The only two who didn't charge anything at an impossible place on an appropriate day were Kim and Murphy."

"That's weird, indicted because they didn't leave a trail? You say one of their executives had his fortune told?"

"Yeah, Willis Lee. He's a top Daewoo salesman, earns a couple of hundred thousand most years."

I was down to the income and asset entries in the Kim and Murphy files, very impressive. "If the motive for the murders was money, that lets these guys out. Both of them are well into six figures."

George left the window and came to loom over me, his yellow aloha shirt just a little brighter than the sunlight he blocked.

"Nah, you're thinking backward again. If a guy is trying to squeak by on forty-fifty thousand, like some people I know, he knows his limits and doesn't usually get in much trouble. Start earning around a quarter million, you get to thinking there aren't any limits, and first thing you know you're in the soup."

"Nice soup. Should I be glad we're not tempted?" The final entry on the sheets was residence addresses. Kim had a condo in that new high-rise on South King Street, the one they call "One Archer Lane," but he also had a home and family in Seoul. Murphy had an address on Kahala Avenue, which likely meant over a million bucks, two million if it was on the ocean side of the street.

I shuffled the papers back together and handed them to George. It was hard for me to imagine having addresses like those by legal means, but then I don't have much experience with quarter-million-dollar annual incomes.

"Did Maggie tell you who her creepy guy was?"

George sat back at his desk, picked up the no-longer-steaming coffee, and put his feet up again. "She said something about the ATF, but forgot the name."

"It was DEA, Spencer, specifically, and Maggie is right, he is one creepy character if you don't know him. Do you suppose his snooping around the islands has anything to do with Darren's murder?"

"I don't see how. You don't really think he was following Maggie?"

"No, when Maggie and I saw him I started to introduce them, but he wasn't the least interested in Maggie. Pure coincidence, probably. So, Sherlock, what's our next move?"

"I thought maybe you'd like to do some moonlighting for the phone company?"

That's when I noticed that George had the FM receivers set up on the copier table.

Chapter 17

No, it is not legal, don't even ask. If we got caught at it, we'd certainly lose our licenses, possibly get the electric chair, but you gotta do what you gotta do. I rented the pickup from Avis, stuck the magnetic "Verizon" signs on the doors, stopped by Honolulu Rents for a couple of ladders, and parked behind the condo high rise at One Archer Lane. I had no intention of using the ladders, they just made the truck look more authentic.

Archer Lane is actually the entrance to the Hawaiian Electric Company yard, one block long, but apparently the address sounds classier than King Street. A couple of furniture moving vans were parked behind the building and a stream of roustabouts carried paper-wrapped treasures in, but there were no phone company trucks parked there.

One good thing about Hawaii is that no one is much into uniforms. I hefted a toolbox and found a security guard sneaking a smoke outside the service entrance. He was wearing a sharp blue uniform and badge, but wasn't surprised that I wasn't. He looked like the friendly type, maybe a superannuated bus driver, but taking his job seriously.

I said, "Phone company." He unlocked the utility room door that fronts on the alley. I snapped on the light and went in; he closed the door and apparently continued to smoke outside.

Phone lines came up out of a conduit in a cable two inches in diameter, and fanned out on two sheets of plywood that were attached to the wall. Very few pairs were labeled, but the wires were laid out logically in rows. Kim's apartment was 2104, so I counted up 21 rows, and the fourth pair over was orange with a white tracer. I was just about to clip the transmitter onto that pair when I realized there weren't nearly enough rows. Specifically, there were thirty-thee rows, and this was a forty-two-story building.

The first row, which had four phones on it and pairs labeled "fire department" and "security," was obviously the lobby area. After that, every row had eight pairs, which nicely matched eight apartments per floor, just not enough rows.

One Archer is the sort of security building that you don't even get into the lobby without a good reason. I picked out a couple of screwdrivers and a pair of long-nosed pliers, left the door to the utility room unlocked, and went looking for the security guard again. He'd finished his cigarette and was watching the furniture movers work.

"Seems to be a problem with the phone at the security desk. Mind if I have a look?"

He shrugged. "It was working all right a while ago."

"Yeah, it is now, but I'm getting a trouble light, probably just a loose wire." He straightened his tie and led the way past a couple of guys who were struggling with a paper-wrapped object the size of a davenport, and into the sacrosanct lobby.

Potted palms, mailboxes, leather couches, a faux marble floor, big mirrors, indirect lighting, and glassed-in cubicles for the manager and a secretary, were all very impressive. The security desk was just inside the front door—open with pass card—and twenty feet across the shining blond faux marble from the bank of three elevators. The right-hand elevator stood with the door open and quilted blankets hanging to protect the finery. The two roustabouts were busily standing the davenport on end in that one. The other two elevators were on high floors and had big, lighted enunciators over the doors.

The guard pointed to the phone on the security desk and gave me another shrug, then headed back outside, either to enjoy the sunshine or sneak another cigarette. I unplugged the phone, flipped it over, and removed the two screws that hold the case. That revealed a suitably bewildering mass of wires. I perched on the edge of the desk and made a show of checking wires for the benefit of the power-dressed and carefully coiffed secretary who was glowering at me from her glass cage.

An elevator started down from 39 and I watched the enunciator. One important question was what happens between fourteen and twelve, and that was nothing. The old superstition was alive and well, the building has no thirteenth floor. The elevator stopped on eleven, passed nine, and the next floor was P-6, the parking garage. Pause there, down to P-2, another pause, past P-1 and the door opened on the lobby.

Chapter Seventeen

An elderly Japanese couple, dressed casual chic, trudged across the lobby, dodged the movers, and checked their mail. I put the phone back together, replaced the cord, listened to the dial tone, and gave the secretary a big smile. She shook her head, maybe waking up from a daydream, and concentrated on her desk.

Counting one, nine through twelve, and fourteen to twenty-one seemed right, but I counted on up anyhow, floor forty-one, penthouse, and the pairs came out right. I clipped the transmitter onto the fourth pair on twenty-one. The transmitter is battery operated, the size of two packs of cigarettes end to end. I clipped the antenna wire to one side of a pair that I figured went to the penthouse. With a little luck, there would be enough unshielded cable on the top floor to radiate some signal. It was simpler in the old days, but now all the cables downtown are underground so you can't radiate from the shield the way we used to when the lines were overhead.

I shut off the light, cracked the door and peeked out. A truck emblazoned Carrier Air Conditioning was trying to sneak between the furniture movers, but the only phone company truck was mine. I slipped out, waved to the air conditioning guy. He backed off and I gave him my parking spot.

King Street is a six-lane, one-way artery leading out of town, but at nine-thirty on a typically glorious sunny morning, four lanes were in use, with cars parked in the outside lanes and delivery trucks in front of the restaurants. The outside lanes are signed: "Tow Away: 3:30-6:30" and they are. By three twenty, cop cars and wreckers will be lined up along the street, and at the stroke of three-thirty they start ticketing and towing. That will cost you a hundred bucks, even if you get there in time to chase your car down the street. I expect the city makes a good bit of money that way, but in this case it is justified because by four, traffic will be gushing from gutter to gutter with people eager to get out of town.

In early spring, King Street is just a pleasant ride past cemeteries, parks, schoolyards and little clusters of suburban businesses, with the basic color scheme green. Not that you aren't seeing flowers. Anytime you look up, anywhere in Hawaii, you will always see flowers, but the prevalent ones in early spring are hibiscus, plumeria, bougainvillea, ginger, stuff like that.

From June through August, driving through that area is almost painfully beautiful. The green trees I was driving under will turn into flame, or poincianas, and shower trees, so loaded with blossoms that

The Dealership

you can't see the leaves, and the whole street will look like a pink, white, yellow, and scarlet confectioner's fantasy, with blossoms drifting down like snowflakes the whole summer.

King Street dumped me onto the freeway and I screeched off again in the Kahala district where one-bedroom homes start at a million-five. Twice as many flowers. With prices like that, I suppose even springtime comes earlier. Kahala Avenue runs along the ocean with one layer of walled estates blocking the view.

Murphy's place was on the ocean side. An eight-foot-tall stone wall, with a steel gate and a number fronted the street, but the phone lines were overhead. I strapped on the climbing hooks and the belt and climbed the pole next to the phone company's breakout box.

There are tricks to that. I suppose every human endeavor has tricks. When you're climbing a pole, the main trick is to use your climbing belt the way it's designed, the bale around the pole to hold yourself on. If you go with your instincts, and try to hold onto the pole with your hands, the angle of your spurs, or hooks, will be straight up and down, not digging in. Lean back against the bale and flip it up as you go so your spurs dig in at a flat angle. If your spurs slip and you slide down the pole, linemen call that maneuver "skinning the pole," but it isn't the pole that gets skinned.

What's called the phone box is actually a rubberized boot, three feet long and six inches in diameter, that clips over the hundred-pair cable. Inside are a cable splice and a terminal block with local phones coming out in single pairs. The pair I was after followed the trunk line for one pole, then went down the pole in conduit and disappeared underground into Murphy's compound. I clipped the transmitter to the terminal block and closed the boot over it. No problem with the antenna on that one.

Those transmitters have VOX, or voice operated circuits, so they only transmit when someone is talking. That makes it unlikely that the Federal Communications Commission, or anyone else, will notice them, and even if they're noticed, they'll be hard to find. The FCC finds illegal transmitters by triangulation, but that can only be done when the transmitter is on, so getting two or three directional fixes on these would take a lot of patience. If they were found, they'd certainly be confiscated, but there was nothing about them pointing to us. You cannot triangulate a receiver.

From the pole, I could see over the stone wall into a bamboo jungle with glimpses of a very large, single-story house, attached garage,

Chapter Seventeen

and hints of beach and ocean beyond. Murphy, and his neighbors for half a mile in each direction, were stretching Hawaiian law a bit. All beaches on Hawaii are public, but the law doesn't mandate providing public access, so the public was welcome to walk on that beach, if they could get there.

I climbed down, dumped the climbing gear in the pickup, rubbed the sore spots on my calves where the steel shanks had dug into them, returned the rented equipment, and went back to the office to see if George was receiving phone calls.

He wasn't, probably because both Kim and Murphy were still at work, and the suspense was killing him. It's even possible that he wasn't one hundred percent confident that I had bugged the right lines and remembered to turn on the transmitter switches. I picked up the notes from his desk and dialed Kim's number. The ring that burst out of George's speakers nearly deafened us. He jerked the volume control down to half before the next ring, and I hung up before we got an answer.

He had already adjusted the other volume while I was dialing Murphy. One half a ring, and the phone said: "Murphy residence."

"Sorry, wrong number," I mumbled.

The outer office door closed with a bang, indicating that the clock had made the last tick to five, and Maggie had escaped. George took his cup to the coffeepot, tipped the pot to get the dregs, and unplugged it. He was settling down to wait for phone calls. I'd had enough of phones, and my arches were killing me. I could still feel the steel shanks of those climbing hooks trying to amputate my feet. I ducked out.

Chapter 18

When I walked past Maude's apartment on the third floor of the Commodore, she was standing at the window, possibly watching teams in war canoes practicing their paddling on the Ala Wai Canal below us, but more likely waiting for me to get home. She waved and rushed to open the door. I backed up and stuck my head in.

"Hi, Dick, hard day at the office? You're looking positively exhausted since Betty left. Come in, come in, have a glass of Betty's favorite Pouilly Fuissé."

I sat on the rail, back to the canal, to take off my shoes. Normally I'd be wearing loafers that just slip off, but I was wearing lace-up, high-top work boots for the pole climb, and Maude was right, I was beat. Those phone company guys climb thirty poles a day and work on top for eight hours, but I don't think they're really human. Bionic, probably.

Maude was wearing a sharp gray business suit and hose, which meant that this was a very special occasion. She had once confided to Betty that she only wore garters to weddings and coronations. She ushered me to a chair at the dining table next to the window where we could watch the high school teams practicing their canoeing, and set a frosty glass of wine on a folded washcloth. Using washcloths for coasters is a Hawaiian trick because the glasses weep about as much moisture down the outside as there is on the inside.

Maude was flitting even more than usual, and when she finally brought her own glass with coaster and joined me at the table, she was still bouncing around.

Maude was too excited to sip. "I talked to Betty today."

I was suddenly sucker-punched right in the solar plexus and very nearly sprayed my first sip of wine back out. The image of Betty that sprang up grabbed me with a physical pain. Blue-green sapphire eyes, always sparkling with fun or mischief, strawberry bob floating

Chapter Eighteen

around her like sunshine, an animated covergirl smile I could watch fascinated forever, and many more, but private assets.

"Betty phoned?" I'd been studiously not conjuring that image since Betty left, and calling it up was like sandpapering a wound.

"Not exactly. I called her. You see, Dick, I've come down with a terrible case of island fever, and I simply have to go to the mainland for a while."

"Maudie, you with island fever? You've been here thirty years and loved every moment of it."

"That's just the point. Supposing a tidal wave came up the canal right now? It's happened to Hilo twice, so we might be next."

"Maude, just how much wine have you drunk?"

"Don't be silly, Dick, and don't argue with me. I've made up my mind, I simply must be in a place where I can drive more than an hour in one direction."

That statement had a familiar ring to it, but the image of Maude driving anywhere at all distracted me. Maude has had a senior bus pass for as long as I can remember, and even navigating by bus was beginning to stretch her abilities.

I reluctantly tucked the image of Betty back into its cubbyhole and felt again the terrible sense of loss. I took a deep breath, steeled my resolve, and braved another sip of the wine. It was cool, delicious, and went straight to the thirst. That's when I noticed Maude's suitcase sitting just inside the door.

"Drink up, Dick, don't dawdle. You need to take me to the airport as soon as you shower off that dreadful aroma you're wearing."

I chugged the wine, terrible waste, scooped my shoes off the lanai and went next door to do as I was told. Maude occasionally accepted input at the early stages of a decision, but once she said the magic words, "I've made up my mind," that was the end of discussion. It was patronizing of me to worry about her because she had circumnavigated the globe twice before I was born. However, she did occasionally get lost in the wilds of the Ala Moana Shopping Center.

The shower felt wonderful, and I started to smell better even to myself. George was probably still perched in the office waiting for a phone to pick up, but he'd get tired of that after a while and defect to the beach house where Monica was, no doubt, waiting with open arms and cold heels. He had a cassette recorder hooked to each receiver and they were also VOX operated, so any calls made overnight would be waiting for us in the morning.

The Dealership

Maude was waiting with her door open, wearing a little round blue hat with an aura of gauze around it and what looked like tiny blue gnats caught in the net. She carefully stepped into matching high-heeled shoes, using the doorknob to keep her balance. I scooped her suitcase off the carpet and followed her. She almost ran down the stairs.

I was having a serious *déjà vu* attack. I had scooped Betty's suitcase off that same carpet, and she too had run down the stairs ahead of me. The difference was that Betty had cried all the way down the stairs and all the way to the airport; Maude was beaming like Christmas morning. She leaned forward in her seat, maybe to get to the airport sooner, and bounced around like a kid with a terrible need for a bathroom.

I parked and carried the suitcase in to the United Airlines desk. Maude was spilling credit cards, tissues, old letters, various female accoutrements on the counter, and finally retrieved her Hawaiian picture ID. I was relieved to note no driver's license. More *déjà vu* in Stinger Ray's, except this time we were sipping wine while Maude went over my list of instructions for the third time: "Collect the mail, water the orchids, close the windows if it looks like rain."

I assured her that I could handle that. When the 747 was shoved away from the gate, Hawaii lost a good bit of its sparkle. I resisted the urge to bang my head against the wall, started to kick one of the concrete planters, but remembered in time that I was wearing loafers. No place else can be as joyous or as lonely as an airport.

Chapter 19

I'd been walking along Ala Moana Beach holding Betty's hand, swinging our hands companionably. Moonlight sparkled a path across the water and reflected green from Betty's eyes when she stopped and turned to me for a kiss. As always, her body melted against me, fitting exactly the way God intended, making that full feeling that this is right, this is perfect, this is what life is for. I hugged her hard, trying to convey my love. Betty gave a shrill little scream and melted. My arms went right through her.

I got the phone on the fourth ring, feeling for it in the dark.

"Dick, Sally. Someone just shot Hiro."

"I'll be there in five minutes." I hung up the phone and groped my way into the shower. I'd been sleeping naked; there is no air conditioning in the Commodore. It took one minute to wash the cobwebs out, and unfortunately the last vestiges of Betty with them, another minute to dress, and I ran for the parking lot. I slipped my wristwatch on while I bounded down the stairs and it said four.

Chamber's Chambers was lit up like noon with portable floodlights. I swung into the drive and immediately shuddered to a halt against the hibiscus hedge while an ambulance bulled past me, turning on lights and cranking up its siren. That was a good sign. Things are bad when the ambulance isn't in a hurry.

A young cop, resplendent in uniform, bristling with guns and badges, stopped me at the top of the drive with an imperious gesture. He was gesturing with a flashlight that looked as big as a baseball bat in his left hand, and his right hand was hovering an inch from his service revolver. For the two seconds it took him to stride down the drive, my lights were in his eyes. I jerked the wallet out of my pocket, ripped my badge out, and dropped the wallet in my lap.

By the time he reached me, I had rolled down the window and

held my badge out, palm up. You do not want anything bigger in your hand. To a cop, particularly a young one, a cell phone or a wallet is apt to look like a gun. He checked out the badge, but managed to keep that thousand-watt flashlight in my eyes.

"Show me some ID." He was nervous, unless his voice was still changing from puberty.

Very slowly, I picked up my wallet with thumb and index finger, letting it hang down like a dead rat by the tail, and passed it out to him. He took the wallet, checked my private eye license, then my driver's license, and compared the pictures on each to me, all the while keeping the flashlight beam solidly in my eyes. I was tempted to reach for my sunglasses, but reaching seemed to be contraindicated. I squinted, and it wasn't much worse than looking at the noonday sun. I did not point out to him that he was breaking a basic rule of police procedure. A cop is never supposed to take your wallet, he's supposed to ask you to remove the ID. That's just in case the question of a missing hundred-dollar bill comes up later. I was obeying an even more basic rule: "The guy with the gun calls the shots."

"Get out, slowly, and keep your hands in sight." He stepped back. Out of the corner of my seriously injured eyes, I could see him draw his pistol. I made it out, apparently to his satisfaction.

"Hands on the car." I didn't make him ask me to "spread 'em," I leaned and spread. He must have put the gun away because he still held the flashlight in position to brain me while he frisked me. I wasn't carrying because my Beretta was still in my desk drawer. Keeping it there was a habit I was going to have to change, but just at the moment it was a good thing.

"Get away from the car." He didn't specify how far, and I had spotted Lieutenant Cochran looming over the activity twenty feet away. I walked over to join Cochran, gambling that the rookie wouldn't shoot me in the back with the lieutenant in the line of fire.

Cochran always looms over crowds, because he's six-foot-five, not counting the shock of rumpled brown hair that indicated he'd been called out of bed. He was wearing a light tweedy sport coat, dark slacks, white shirt sans tie. The coat was open, but mandatory to cover the .45 automatic in his shoulder holster. He was supervising a crew that was fitting wooden dowels into bullet holes in the garage door.

No need to ask what happened. The line of bullet holes started at the left edge of the door, hole every six inches, then a gap about as wide as Hiro, and the stitched holes continued across the door.

Chapter Nineteen

It looked like four bullet holes were missing, so those bullets were probably in Hiro. An ominous pool of blood reflected light on the pavement to the right of the missing holes. The dowels in the bullet holes all pointed to the right at the same angle.

"He was shooting from that rise in the bamboo thicket across the lawn."

Cochran spun around. "How the hell do you know, Payne? Were you here, or did you do the shooting?"

"Tricks of the detective trade," I told him. "When you get around to check, you'll find motorcycle tracks at the bottom of the rise next to the road."

Cochran whistled for the sentry who had tried to blind me, gave him some terse—but too quiet to hear—instructions, and the kid trotted down the lane, following his flashlight.

"How bad is Hiro hurt?" I asked.

"He'll live, thanks to the body armor he was wearing, but he's got some broken ribs, and that blood is his. Must have been hit in the shoulder. He was cursing and fighting too much for a guy with a head wound."

"Did he shoot back?"

"I'd say so. We had to take an empty .357 away from him. It's confiscated at the moment, in case we find someone wandering around with bullet holes."

"What the heck was he, or us for that matter, doing out here at four in the morning?"

"Other than getting shot, he was checking because an alarm went off. Mrs. Chambers had a perimeter alarm installed. Apparently there was a shooter here once before."

"Really?" I asked. "Anybody hurt that time?"

"Cute, Payne, very cute. Why don't you just tell me that you've been hanging around ever since her husband was killed? We could use you for a suspect if you're having a thing with the missus, not that I'd blame you."

The rookie came trotting up the drive, nodding his head. He didn't have enough breath left to speak. He bent over, bracing his hands on his knees and just gasped for a while. There's something about running uphill.

"My relationship with Mrs. Chambers is strictly professional. I never even heard of her before her husband was shot."

"Is that right? That explains why the two of you checked into a love nest at the Tapa Tower. But maybe that doesn't count if she called herself Mrs. Payne and wore a brunette wig? Don't you want to go in and hold her hand? She's a little upset at the moment." Cochran turned his back on me and strode over to his unmarked car. It was one of the blue Plymouths that make up Honolulu's fleet of identical unmarked cars. Folding his bulk into that car reminded me of closing a pocketknife, but he was slamming the car door when I ran past him and up the walk to the front porch.

The front door was open, and so was the door to the second room down the hall. A drape had been pulled across the windows to that room so I couldn't see in until I got to the door. Vanessa was standing just inside the door, sharp blue uniform, dark blue necktie over light blue shirt, and sergeant's stripes on her shoulder. The jacket was short so it didn't cover the gun and handcuffs attached to her oversized belt.

She had turned toward the door when she heard me in the hall, but she wasn't going for her gun. The difference between Vanessa and the rookie, other than the obvious physical attributes, was that Vanessa wasn't scared. It would take a lot more than a line of bullet holes across a garage door, and a wounded bodyguard, to rattle Vanessa's stolid Nordic psyche.

"Hi, Dick, in here." She motioned with a flick of her short blonde bob, keeping the expression on her pretty face neutral. I tried to read some camaraderie in her steady blue eyes. I've always liked Vanessa. She's a good cop and doesn't wear that defensive chip on her shoulder that so many females have when they enter a predominately male profession. That may be partly because she doesn't need one. She could have been the first female linebacker on a pro football team if she'd wanted to. I cherish the notion that she liked me, too, but her neutral expression conveyed that she wouldn't hesitate to clap the cuffs on me if that were warranted.

Vanessa and I go back a long ways together: specifically, to the day we shared a chunk of concrete sewer pipe two feet high and four feet long. We were behind the pipe, not in it, but it was pretty crowded and anything that had stuck out would have been shot off. A highly irate ex-employee of a local business was in a second floor window spraying our sewer pipe with automatic fire, and our pipe sounded like the last hurrah of one of those Chinese firecracker strings. When the perp ran out of ammunition, we both jumped out and shot. He did a swan dive out of the window, and when they picked up the corpse there were two bullet holes in his forehead: one .38 and one .32.

Chapter Nineteen

That made quite a problem for the bureaucracy. There's a clear procedure to follow when an officer kills someone, and an even more stringent one when a private detective does, no matter how obvious the case for self-defense may be. Their problem was that only one of us could have killed him; the other just mutilated a corpse a millisecond later, and they couldn't tell which was which. I expected them to throw the book at both of us, but that time they backed off and gave us both the benefit of the doubt.

Sally sat on a low couch, hugging herself, almost rocking like an autistic child. Her hair was mussed and there were tear streaks down her cheeks. When she saw me, she jumped up, threw her arms around my neck, buried her face in my shoulder, and bawled like the world was ending. I hugged her back, and I'm ashamed to say that she felt quite a lot like Betty did in the same sort of clinch. For one thing, Sally was wearing a long white tee shirt and apparently nothing else, so it was pretty damned intimate.

The maid came in carrying a tray with coffee cups and a silver pitcher. She was wearing a blue bathrobe, but when she bent to set the tray on the coffee table it was obvious that she was naked under the robe. It wasn't prurient; this was a more basic situation. It was like those women who run out of a burning building naked, or run straight from a shower to a busy street during an earthquake. Clothes are a secondary consideration. When it comes to survival, they don't count.

Vanessa was taking in the scene, and watching me take in the scene, but she wasn't drawing the off-color conclusions that Cochran would have. I think Sally was belting out not so much grief over Hiro as anger and frustration at the whole episode, and her hugging me wasn't personal. I think at that moment she was hugging a father figure, or maybe vicariously leaning on the deceased Darren.

Floodlights in the driveway were switched off. I heard a generator stop and a car engine start. A minute later, a car horn beeped. Vanessa backed out of the room, then turned and strode down the hall. The maid had disappeared, so it was just Sally and me standing there, hugging like Romeo and Juliet. I felt Sally register the situation and stiffen. It was okay to be hugging me with the cops in attendance, a little different when we were alone.

Sally eased out of the embrace. She started to use the hem of her tee shirt to wipe her eyes, but realized that wasn't such a good idea. I handed her my handkerchief.

"Thanks, Dick. Care for coffee?"

Chapter 20

"You'll stay?"

"I'll stay. Show me how to work the alarms."

Sally led the way down the dark hallway toward the garage. We stepped into the connecting room between the house and the garage, and Sally turned on an overhead light. I watched her realize that she was functionally naked, then decide that it didn't matter anymore.

The back wall had a mounted switch panel. Switches were marked *perimeter, motion, proximity*. A red light next to the perimeter alarm was flashing, and next to that, another red light was marked *alarm silence*. Sally punched the button labeled *reset* and both lights went out. The motion switch was turned off. Sally frowned and turned that one on.

"Why do you suppose Hiro turned off the alarms?" Sally asked. "A siren should have gone off when the perimeter was breached."

"Because he realized you were being invaded, wanted to surprise the shooter, and didn't want to disturb you. He just misjudged how fast the shooter could get up the hill."

"You won't make a mistake like that, will you, Dick?"

"Not a chance. Hiro was being a hero; I'm your basic coward and you may count on that. Go back to bed. I'm going to hang out here and walk down the hall now and then."

"Okay, the room where you met us tonight is my personal sitting room. My bedroom is through the door at the back of that room."

"Bedroom windows?" I asked.

"Solid glass, but they overlook the city with several hundred feet of sheer cliff below them."

"Where does the maid sleep?"

"She's in the first room past the front door, same layout as mine."

"And Hiro?"

Chapter Twenty

"He has his own apartment over the garage."

"Okay, got it. Lock both of your doors and go to bed. You'll probably hear me walk down the hall every few minutes. Don't worry about it."

"Thanks, Dick." She started to hug me, flashed again on her state of undress, and backed out of the room. She gave me a self-conscious little wave, turned and fled. I did not watch her run down the hall.

Hiro's apartment over the garage had a front room with a row of windows overlooking the parking apron, and a bedroom at the back with a view of Honolulu's lights. His bath was neat, clean towels on the rack by the shower and, I was surprised to note, a shower cap hanging by the taps. He had a kitchen off the front room, everything clean and put away, no hint of what he'd had for dinner. I tossed the apartment fast, but kept it neat. I was looking for a gun. I hadn't told Sally that I didn't have one with me, so I was there under false pretenses, and feeling pretty naked besides. It had occurred to me that the shooter knew Hiro had been hit, so once the police left, this was the perfect time to come back.

I'd checked all the likely places and was getting a little panicky until I found the cardboard box under the bed. It was three inches thick, eight inches wide, and three feet long. The picture on the box was a cowboy riding a bucking bronco and brandishing a rifle.

When you toss an apartment, you can expect embarrassment. Maybe it's a collection of pornography or even props for bondage and discipline. Maybe it's a packet of love letters, maybe female undergarments in an all-male environment, whatever. There are bound to be secrets and you expect them, even accept them with minimal judgment, but discovering Hiro's secret punctured even my facade of urbanity. I felt so badly, such a keen sense of the privacy invaded, that I would have put the box back if I hadn't been desperate.

When I pulled the lid off the box, the piles of papers on top were used targets: bull's eyes, twelve inches in diameter. The first pile had been perforated minimally with the .357 magnum pistol, two or three holes to the target and all of them in the outer rim or on the paper, clear outside the ring. The next pile was better, ten shots to the target and several of them within the rings, but the holes were tiny, and the reason for that was underneath the targets.

It was a rifle all right, a Red Ryder BB gun. Not a Daisy air rifle, not a pellet gun, but the sort of BB gun you give your kid for his fifth birthday, powered by a spring. I jerked it out, checked that the

109

tube was full of BBs, and slid the box back under the bed, but my number two priority, after not getting shot, was to get that rifle back under the bed before Hiro discovered my prying. If he found out that anyone had seen those targets, he'd be so embarrassed that one of us would have to leave the island.

Come to think of it, if I was caught patrolling the premises with a BB gun, Hiro and I might leave together. I carried the rifle across my arm as if it weighed ten pounds instead of one, and tromped down stairs to make myself into a target. The alarms were all on, all lights green, nothing blinking. I strolled down to the end of the hall and back, mostly to let Sally hear me on patrol, if she was still awake.

Just enough light from a half-hearted moon and the ambience of the city turned the lawn a dusky gray with inky black shadows next to the house and under every tree. The bamboo curtain was moving, but in waves from trade winds, not jerks from shooters. The house side of the hall was dark. I didn't try the doors, but they looked locked until I got to the patio. The window of the former shooting gallery had been replaced. White cobblestones around the pool seemed to glow with an eerie greenish phosphorescent light. City sounds were muffled, what passes for silence in Honolulu, which meant that just for that moment, I didn't hear any sirens.

Between patrols, I checked Hiro's windows. All of them could be opened and the screens were the type you unclip from inside. I de-screened one front window and one over the chasm behind the house. I leaned out of the back one to check Sally's "unapproachable" theory. She was right, I was looking straight down several hundred feet. It was still too dark to make out details, but streetlights appeared to be directly below me and very small.

After my next walk down the dark hallway, I varied the routine by checking the garage. The inside of the first door had some serious splinters where the bullets had come in, and the limousine was parked right inside it. It hadn't occurred to me that the limo would have bulletproof glass, but it did. Three white check marks on the rear window, and one on the side near the front, showed where bullets had been deflected. A couple of holes in the ceiling from ricochets finished that scenario. A case of oil on a bench along the back wall had an ugly tear in it and two or three quarts of oil had leaked out onto the floor, but the thing that struck me was that the limo was the only car in a three-car garage. I suddenly realized that Darren's car hadn't been accounted for.

By six-thirty, it was getting light, and I'd made enough trips down

Chapter Twenty

the hall. I turned off the light in Hiro's apartment and settled down in the open front window where I had a view down the drive and across the road. In less than five minutes a car went by, going up the hill, way too slowly for my taste. Three minutes later, the same car came back the other way, barely creeping past the drive. I broke all the rules, flipped on the light so I could be seen, and made a show of aiming the rifle at the car. Tires screamed and he was gone, apparently not stopping to wonder why I had turned on the light. I switched it off again and let the clock creep to seven before I called George.

The muzzy "Hello" was definitely not George.

"Hi, Monica, this is Dick."

"Who's Dick?"

"Dick, Dick, George's partner, I need to speak to him."

I could still hear Monica but she was not talking to me.

"George, wake up. It's an obscene phone call. Tell him there's a man here."

Much mumbling, springs creaking, "What the hell do you want?"

"Good morning, George, I trust you slept well?"

"Dick? What's the idea of getting Monica all shook up? Why the hell are you calling in the middle of the night?"

"Sorry, next time I'll tell her it's Mr. Payne calling. You guys don't play any S & M games, do you? Anyhow, I need a gun and I need one fast. Any chance of your getting up before noon?"

"What's going on?" George suddenly sounded awake.

"I'm at Chambers' Chambers, guarding the fort. There was another attack last night. Hiro got shot, and I'm up here pointing my finger at the bad guys and saying, 'bang, you're dead.'"

"Fifteen minutes. Monica, where the hell are my pants? Cut that out, this is serious."

"When you get here, stop on the road and blink your lights a couple of times. I need to shut off some alarms before you start up the drive."

"Not my pajama pants, dummy, the pair you hid when I came home. I'm on the way." Click.

It was fourteen minutes. When George blinked his lights I ran down, shut off the alarms, turned on a porch light, and opened the pedestrian door onto the drive. George swung into the drive, zipped up the hill and jumped out.

"I thought you said you didn't have a weapon."

I handed him the Red Ryder rifle, butt first.

"What in the hell is that?" George held the BB gun up to the porch light trying to believe what his eyes were telling him. "Where did you get that? Pointing your finger was a much better plan."

"Believe me, you don't want to know. Got any other ideas?"

George ducked back into the car and handed me the 9mm Glock that was on the seat. I stuck the Glock in my belt and rescued Red Ryder from George before he tossed it into the bushes. The Glock is George's favorite, the classic model 17. It's got to be the ugliest gun ever made, but it is fast becoming the most popular. It has that polymer frame—never call it plastic—so it weighs less than a pound, but the seventeen 9mm bullets in the clip give it a nice heft. It's seven inches long, just a bit too much for a pocket, but they managed to squeeze a four-and–a-half-inch barrel into that, so it's accurate by semiautomatic standards.

"How is Hiro?" George asked.

"Why don't you drive down to Straub Hospital and find out? He was wearing a bulletproof vest, but they shot him with something pretty heavy and he's leaking blood." I pointed. The puddle of blood had turned black, but it was still impressive.

"You going to be all right?"

"I am now." I patted the Glock, and it felt good. "Come back in an hour with a report on Hiro, and we'll get Sally up."

George nodded, pulled a U-turn and disappeared down the hill. I went back inside and found Sally staring at the alarm panel. She was dressed, dark slacks and white blouse, and her expression much more formal than the one I was remembering.

"Dick, you shut off the alarms. You promised."

"Just two minutes ago, I had to let George in and I didn't want him setting them off."

"George is here?"

"No, he's gone to check on Hiro." I reached past Sally and made a show of switching the alarms back on. Mostly I was trying to keep the BB gun out of sight. Sally did not need to know that her bodyguard was trying to learn how to shoot.

"Want to come upstairs while I make coffee?"

"Carmalita already served. I came to invite you."

"Great, I'll be right there." Sally turned back down the hall, I ran upstairs and did my best to replace Hiro's artillery exactly the way I had found it.

Chapter 21

"Where is Darren's car?" I asked.

"Gee, I don't know. I never thought about it." Sally removed a white cloth from the serving tray.

"How did you get to the yacht?"

"Hiro dropped me off, but since I was planning to meet Darren there and spend the evening, Hiro went on home."

"How would Darren normally have got there?"

"He would have driven his Mercedes, but it wasn't in the lot, or I would have noticed it and known that Darren was there."

"Mind if I use your phone?"

"Of course not." Sally sat down on the couch, poured two cups of coffee and slid chunks of a freshly baked coffeecake onto saucers.

I grabbed the phone off the end table, dialed police headquarters, and took a sip of my coffee while I waited for Cochran.

"Cochran here." He always sounded as if the caller was his worst enemy and calling at the most inconvenient time.

"Cochran, Payne. Got a clue for you to follow up since you're not busy."

"It better be good."

"It is. Darren Chambers' car is missing. He almost certainly drove it to the dock with the killer in it, and the killer left in the car after the deed. Might be instructive to find the car."

Cochran hung up on me, but that meant he hadn't thought about the car either. If he had, he'd have blistered my ear with the triviality of my thinking. Naturally, he didn't thank me; that's a word not in his vocabulary.

Sally and I sat in her living room, drinking rich, black coffee and each of us nibbling the edges of our chunks of coffeecake. It wasn't a time for banter and neither of us was about to refer to the night before. It was a relief when the siren let out a low wail. I ran down the hall and shut off the perimeter alarm, but left the others on while George drove up the incline.

He'd come twenty feet when the motion sensors picked him up and let out a series of beeps like a truck's backing up. I shut off that one and waited to see what the proximity alarm would do. George parked the car, got out and tromped up the walk. He was ten feet from the front door when the alarms started a hee-haw screech like those police vehicles in foreign movies. I shut off the proximity alarm and turned the perimeter back on.

George was standing inside the front door when I came out of the alarm room and motioned him down the hall to Sally's living room. Sally just looked the question to George.

"Hiro's got four broken ribs taped up and a nasty gash on his shoulder, but he's sitting up eating Jello. They'll release him when the doctor comes back on duty and pronounces him infection free, about one o'clock tomorrow. Dick, you remember Celeste? She was your nurse the time you got your prehensile tail shot off?"

"Yeah, I remember Celeste, and thanks for reminding me. There is a point to this conversation?"

"Well, she does send her best regards, but she's in charge of the shift now. She whispered what's going on. If they release Hiro in less than twenty-four hours and he develops an infection they could be liable for malpractice, so there he stays until tomorrow afternoon. Not his idea, he wanted to come with me. Got up and tromped to the closet to get dressed, but his clothes were missing. His options were to come home in that backless gown or go back to bed. Is there coffee left in that pot?" George set a portable cassette recorder on the end of the coffee table and plunked himself down in the easy chair.

Sally poured a cup for George and scooped a piece of the coffeecake onto a saucer. George picked up the cup, a napkin, and the cake, ignored the forks, and dug in. Nothing wrong with his appetite. He scarfed down the cake, swiped his cheeks with the napkin, and reached to collect another chunk of the cake. He did manage a sip of his coffee before he attacked the second hunk.

When he slowed down a little, I pointed to the cassette recorder. "I gather you got some phone calls?"

George had the grace to swallow before he spoke. "Little problem there, the calls are all in Korean. I'll take them to Fat Fat when it opens, someone there will translate."

Chapter Twenty-One

Sally pouted into the same expression she had when she noticed that I had turned off the alarms. "You've been making illegal phone taps?"

"Sally," I set my cup down and tried to look respectable, "there are two kinds of phone taps. The ones you're thinking of require a court order and can be used as evidence. The ones we made are called 'exploratory,' for our information only, and are used while a case is being developed." That was a crock, and Sally knew it, but she did nod her head so I continued. "At this point we have two prime suspects but no hard evidence, so desperate measures are justified."

Sally was still nodding, but not in agreement. Her nod just meant she had decided to play along. "Maybe I can help. I don't really speak Korean, but I've picked up quite a bit around the office."

George stuffed the last half-bite of cake into his mouth and extracted two cassette tapes from his pocket while he chewed. He inserted a tape into the machine and sipped coffee. "This first call is to Phillip's Takeout." He punched the recorder into play and we listened to the preamble of beeps.

"How do you know who he was calling?" Sally still wasn't much in favor of this caper.

George hit the pause button to explain: "The tones were the number he was calling. I just looked up the number in the reverse phone book." He punched *play* again.

To my ear, the conversation that followed didn't appear to be in words, just a sing-song collection of sounds, but Sally was getting it, and from her expression I thought it was a confession of the murders. It wasn't.

"Hey, that's Harry Kim. Have you guys lost your minds? Harry couldn't possibly be involved; I'd trust him with my life."

"Sally," I said, "that is exactly the point. Both Darren and William Chun trusted their killer. Darren walked down the stairs ahead of him, William was having a drink with him in the living room. We've eliminated over a hundred possible suspects who didn't have the opportunity to commit both murders. These two had the opportunity. What we don't know is any possible motive for them or anyone else. We have to find a motive by whatever means it takes."

"Well, this isn't much of a motive. He's ordering dinner, having kalbi ribs, chicken katsu, seaweed and kim chee."

George shrugged. "Right, that was an innocent call, but the next one may not be. He's calling Korea, but he's schmoozing a dame. If

115

he has a mistress, that's a classic reason to get greedy." George fast-forwarded to the next message and we listened to a long series of beeps. Sally broke in after 20 seconds. "He's schmoozing a dame alright, great motive. His pet name for her happens to be 'mother.'"

George held up placating hands. "Okay, okay, let that one go. This next tape sounds very suspicious. He only made one call, but it was to an electronic surveillance company, and he sounds furious." George had changed the cassettes, punched the second one into play and fast-forwarded past the beeps. Sally listened intently, asked George to rewind a couple of sections, and her mood seemed to be improving.

"Do you want a literal translation?" Sally asked.

"Make it as exact as you can." George reached to pour more coffee, then in a fit of magnanimity, topped off our cups, too.

"Well, you're right, he's angry. He says his housekeeper saw some—now, this word is hard to translate because it refers to bodily elimination processes, but it also means stupid person—she saw this person climb a telephone pole and install a bug on a phone line, then later he called her to test it. He wants that bug removed immediately because he has some important business calls to make. Then he uses that word again, and says they should know that the phone company doesn't climb poles anymore. They use those 'cherry-picker' trucks. The guy he was talking to promised to have the bug removed in half an hour. Anything else you want me to listen to?"

"Wish to heck there was," George said. "Damn, there goes a two-thousand-dollar transmitter."

"Can't you get it back?" Sally asked.

"Oh yeah, we'll get it back. The guy who removed it will offer it for sale. We can stop by his shop and tell him we want to buy one, no problem, but we can't admit that it was ours before." George put the cassettes away and snagged another slab of coffeecake.

"Look, Sally," I said, "here's what we're up against." I poured another cup of the coffee and sat back. I had decided it was time for a lecture. "There are three things required to zero in on a murder suspect: motive, opportunity and means. Taking them backward, the means in this case are all over the map. The .38 revolver is American. The automatic rifle that they shot at Maggie and me on Kauai was a Russian Kalashnikov, very probably the same type of gun that just shot Hiro. That doesn't mean Russians, because every bad guy in the world, and most of the good guys, use Kalashnikovs. The rifle they

Chapter Twenty-One

shot at us with here was a sniper's rifle or hunting rifle, I think a .300 Savage. The reason he missed us is that we were too close. That gun was designed for a hundred yards, and he was trying to use it at a hundred feet. That brings us to the explosion on the yacht. We think the detonator they used was a South Korean army leftover, so that is why we're concentrating on Koreans. Does that make sense?"

Sally was nodding. She had figured out that there was a lecture coming, filled her cup, sat back and crossed her knees, but in the slacks it just wasn't the same as the sundress.

"Okay," I continued, "next is opportunity. Now we know that we're up against an organization, mostly because of the two guys on Kauai who were obviously not the ones that killed Darren and William Chun. Whoever committed those murders was a friend of the victims, a very different situation from the hired hands who are creeping through the bushes. That's why we're concentrating on those two murders, and why we've singled out two men who were friends of both victims and had the opportunity." I was running down, and my coffee was getting cold.

George took over. "So, that brings us to motive, and that is the real puzzler. There are three basic categories of motives. In broad terms, they are revenge, love-sex-or passion, and greed. We're ruling out the twisted love affair, so that leaves revenge or greed. Both are possible, and you are the key to the solution. Probably you know something you shouldn't know, or the killer thinks that you do. I'm not suggesting that you're holding out on us. Whatever it is, you don't realize its importance, or maybe you really don't know it." That was as long as George could go without grabbing another chunk of the cake, so he reached. Sally was sipping regularly, and we still had her attention. I took over.

"If it's revenge, you've got to think back, something that you, Darren, and William Chun were involved in. It may have been years ago, and it needn't be important, except in the killer's mind. We think that is the less likely scenario because of the apparent size of the organization.

"That brings us to greed. Someone stands to make money by getting rid of you, or perhaps continue to make money by a means that you are threatening."

Sally was nodding, but she wasn't having any epiphanies. Actually, she looked like she might burst into tears from sheer frustration. It was time to back off with the theories.

The Dealership

George stood up, scooped his recorder off the table, and drained the last drop from his cup before he set it down. "I'd better check in with the office. I'll bring Hiro home when they release him. Oh, by the way, Dick, I did bring your Beretta. Want to trade it for the Glock?"

"How about I keep both of them? The cops confiscated Hiro's pistol, so he's going to need another one, assuming he's in shape to use it. I thought maybe I'd loan him the Beretta."

George shrugged, and handed over the automatic. He hesitated, very tempted to grab the last piece of the coffeecake and take it with him. I grabbed it to put him out of his misery. George gave me a dirty look and slouched out. I followed him down the hall to operate the alarms.

"You do realize you're stuck here for the night?" George asked.

"Yeah, that had crossed my mind."

"Lucky you've got those alarms, you'll be perfectly safe."

"Yeah. Tell that to Hiro."

Chapter 22

Carmalita served a kind of paella with coos coos and we ate in Sally's living room. Sally had been working at her desk when dinner was served and she kept glancing at the desk while we ate, so when Carmalita gathered up the trays, I excused myself and got out of Sally's way.

Hiro had a good three-cell flashlight stashed in his apartment. I purloined that and felt like an old-time cowboy with the Glock in my belt and the Beretta in my pocket, but I did have to shut off the alarms before I stuck my nose outside. I needed to see exactly where and how those alarms were wired. The proximity alarm looked like a small camera mounted above the garage doors and pointed along the front of the house. The motion sensor was beside it but focused out over the lawn.

I followed the wire down the concrete curb beside the driveway. The perimeter alarm was perched on a palm tree, just high enough to see over the hedge. The lens reminded me of a toy slide projector I had as a kid. It apparently would have seen movement on the back side of the knoll, so that was good. I retreated to the house, turned on the alarms, and used the cover from Hero's bed to make a nest on a chair in front of his windows.

I slept, but woke up every time a car passed, so I was dragging a bit at breakfast. No alarms had rung until George delivered Hiro.

Hiro's left arm was in a sling with some serious bandages on his shoulder. His complexion was lighter than usual, and the skin around his eyes and mouth looked tight, like maybe it had shrunk, but that only accented his expression of grim determination.

We were standing on the lawn and I was explaining the joys of shooting the Beretta. "It's going to take some getting used to, so you can't expect to be as good with it as you are with your .357. The barrel is shorter, and it's lighter, so it's going to feel different.

"If I'm making a difficult shot, and have plenty of time, what I like to do is hold my left arm up like this, and rest the butt of the gun on it. The sights are just like your revolver, but maybe a little more critical because the barrel is shorter."

I demonstrated, holding my left arm up horizontally, crooked at the elbow, Beretta in my right hand with the gun butt resting on my left wrist. "See that top blossom on the hibiscus by the knoll?" The bush I indicated had plenty of dirt behind it, so it was safe to shoot, and it was forty feet away, far enough to demonstrate that the gun was accurate.

"Now, just like your .357, set the front sight in the notch of the rear sight, target on top the sight, and squeeze gently ..." The hibiscus blossom fluttered to the ground. I figured it was important for Hiro to see that the gun really does shoot where you point it. When you're trying to learn to shoot accurately and don't, there's a tendency to think that something is wrong with the gun.

"If I'm shooting fast, or making multiple shots, what I like to do is start with the gun pointed above the target. It's going to kick up between shots, not as much as your .357, but the principle is the same. For instance, if I wanted to shoot those next five blossoms, I'd line up the sights, bring the gun down, and fire when the target goes by."

I snapped off the next five shots in two seconds and the five blossoms were gone. I was showing off, and there was luck involved, but Hiro needed to know what the gun can do, and at least watch how it was done.

"The Tomcat holds seven shots," I said, "so there's one left. Can you raise your left arm high enough with that sling on?" I handed the Beretta to Hiro.

He swung the sling up, rested the gun on his arm, aimed at the next blossom down, and blew it away. The look of happy shock on his face was glorious to behold. I handed him the box of shells and went back to the house. Hiro stayed out there blasting away for the next twenty minutes, and when I sneaked a peek, most of the blossoms were gone from the hibiscus.

The door to Sally's domain was closed, so I wandered out onto the lanai and stretched out on a white rattan recliner by the pool. The sun was warm, but there was just enough breeze for perfect comfort. I closed my eyes, just for a moment ...

When I opened them, Sally was sitting beside me sipping from a tall glass of iced tea, and another glass, apparently for me, sat on the table beside her. I did hope that I hadn't been snoring.

Chapter Twenty-Two

"Sorry to wake you, but Lani just called from Hilo." Sally handed me the glass. The image of Lani in robe and pajamas lying on the floor beside the shotgun leapt to mind, but was quickly supplanted by the memory of her in slacks and sweater giving us a Hawaiian goodbye hug.

Sally continued. "Seems that they had a Daewoo on the lot for a demonstrator. It's missing, and some of the salesmen are saying that her father stole it. They've been out searching Chun's property, and Lani is scared."

"That's crazy," I blurted out. I wasn't quite awake yet, or I wouldn't have been so sure, but that was the answer that Sally wanted to hear.

"Do you think there's a connection with the murders?" she asked.

I grabbed the glass of tea and took a long drink before I answered. "Daewoo is Korean. That's a coincidence, and in Detective School 101 the first lesson is that there are no coincidences. Do you feel safe now that Hiro is back? He's a little banged up, but he seems to be functional."

"You want to go to Hilo?"

I glanced at my watch. "Plenty of time to catch the last flight."

"I thought you would. Yes, I think Hiro is okay. Thanks for teaching him to shoot, by the way."

"What?"

"He's been going to the target range twice a week and coming back looking as if he had been crying. Right now he looks like a cat with a bowl of canaries and cream. I watched your demonstration. You're pretty good with that gun."

"Yeah," I said, "that's the easy part. It's finding out who to shoot that's tough. If you'll excuse me, I've got a plane to catch." I stood up, drank half the tea, and slipped out. It must be something about Sally that brings those macho cracks out of me. I'm usually a pretty modest guy.

I swung by the office. I wanted to get synchronized with George, and give him back his Glock. Maggie looked up with that bright new smile and a cheerful "Hi, Dick." She didn't even seem to be in a hurry to get back to her book.

When I mentioned "Daewoo," George spun around, started punching on his keyboard, and seemed to have tuned me out. "Daewoo" flashed on the screen.

"Hey," I tried to bring him back. "Are you coming to Hilo with me, or not?"

"No need to shout. I'm not deaf, I just can't hear you right now.

The Dealership

Do you realize this is our first real clue? I'm not leaving this computer until I know everything there is to know about Daewoo. Why don't you take Maggie?"

"What?"

"Now you're deaf? I said, if you think you need some backup, take Maggie." George was gone. That computer sometimes seems to suck him in, like Alice through the looking glass. I tossed the Glock on his desk and stomped out.

If my teeth had been false, I would have dropped them when I passed Maggie's desk. She was up, had her jacket on, and her purse in her hand. She snagged my arm when I stormed by. That was the first time it occurred to me that Maggie actually heard what was going on in the office.

"Come on, Dick, lighten up with that scowl; you're going to break your face." I wasn't leading Maggie; she was pulling me, and had already punched the elevator button. "I did okay on Kauai, didn't I? Like you said, we've been shot at together before, so what's the problem?"

"Maggie, sometimes even the bad guys hit what they're shooting at." Maggie was dragging me across the garage toward the Jag. My philosophy is that when something is inevitable, you should deal with it because you can't wish it away. Like, if you're standing in front of a tidal wave, it's best to take a deep breath. Something about Maggie, already in the Jag waiting for me, had the inevitability of a tidal wave, or maybe an avalanche.

It did seem like it might be okay. After all, we weren't headed for a shoot-out with a gang of terrorists. We were going to investigate a car theft, and get Lani calmed down. Maggie might be good at that. Sherlock Holmes had his Dr. Watson, Nero Wolfe had Archie, and where would Perry Mason have been without Della Street? I pulled out of the garage and we survived the first life-threatening stage of the assignment: I got us onto Nimitz Highway, headed toward the airport, without being killed.

Chapter 23

Noelani was dawdling about handing me the keys to a Ford Escort. We do have a fast break number, so the paperwork is all done in advance, but Noelani was taking her time anyway. Today she was wearing white plumeria blossoms in her braid. They set off her dark complexion wonderfully, and the smooth petals draw your attention to how smooth Noelani's skin was, except she had some uncharacteristic lines of suspicion around her eyes. What I didn't like was the quizzical way she kept looking back and forth between Maggie and me.

"Noelani," I said, "this is Detective Margaret Capriccio. She'll be using our account from time to time." That helped. Noelani smiled at Maggie, said, "Hi," and handed me the keys.

We pulled off the highway into the car lot. It was getting dark fast, but the lot appeared to be open. At least the door was open, and the lights were on. When we stepped into the reception area, the only person there was a secretary wearing a dark-blue Hawaiian muumuu. She gave us a cheerful smile at first, but when she realized we weren't customers, she wasn't so friendly. She was tall and skinny—*slender* didn't fit her—somewhere between forty and sixty. If she were merchandise in a supermarket, she'd be in the dried fruit section. Furthermore, I'm pretty sure she was Korean, but she wasn't packing iron.

I asked to see the paperwork on the missing Daewoo, and when that brought a wooden-Indian stare, I flipped out my badge. She reached under the counter, as if she might be going for a gun, but she pulled out a folder and slammed it down on the counter.

"Hey," I said, "we're on the same side here. We want to find out who stole the Daewoo; so do you. We didn't come to cause problems, we came to solve them." She didn't look convinced, and stomped back to sit at her desk. I reached for the folder, but there weren't any papers in it. Maggie had grabbed the papers, and zipped down to the end of the counter. She punched buttons on a complicated keyboard and started feeding the papers into a machine.

Just before I hollered, I figured out that it was not a paper shredder; she was faxing the papers to George. She brought them back to me, one at a time, when the machine spit them out. Some of the stuff made sense. It was a Leganza Sedan, Galaxy White, with a list of standard features as long as the list of forbidden articles on airfreight. It started with air conditioning and alloy wheels, listed everything powered that can be powered, including a sunroof, and ended with traction control and anti-theft. Apparently the anti-theft option hadn't worked.

I tried to imitate the smile that George melts women with, but that didn't work either. "Can you tell us the circumstances of the theft?" I asked the receptionist.

"If you're cops, why don't you read your report?" She stuck a little plastic earphone on her head, turned on a machine, and started typing. I think we were dismissed.

"Can we do that?" Maggie asked. She had shuffled the papers back into a neat pile and reinserted them in the folder. I gave her a half-wink and a so-so hand wobble below the counter.

"Let's go back to headquarters," I said. "No one here is going to cooperate with the police." I stomped out, and Maggie was right behind me. I was trying to convey disgust, but Maggie outdid me tenfold.

I swung the Escort onto the highway, headed toward Mountain View.

"Can we really read the police reports?" Maggie asked.

"In the morning, yes. Right now we have a much more important mission."

I turned the headlight knob, and the lights came on, so already we were having a better trip than the last visit to Mountain View. Now, if Lani didn't meet us with her shotgun ...

The gate was closed, so I got out and gave it a shove. It didn't budge. Then I saw the box with a speaker grille and a button, mounted on a post beside the gate. I pushed the button.

"Who is it?" the box asked.

"Lani, this is Dick." I didn't get any further, the gate buzzed and swung open. I got back in the car, drove through, and was just getting out to close the gate again when it swung shut and went "click" all by itself. I drove up the lane and parked next to Lani's Miata. We were climbing out when the front door banged open and she came bounding down the steps.

Chapter Twenty-Three

"Thank heaven you guys got here. Sally said you were coming …"

Lani registered that Maggie was not George and stopped short, mouth still open.

"Lani, this is Detective Capriccio. Call her Maggie." The two girls eyed each other and decided to be friends.

"Come in, come in." Lani had me by the arm and was pulling. I didn't require any further persuasion. On the lanai, she stopped, looked around, maybe expecting werewolves. She shoved Maggie and me through the door, slammed and locked it. When she turned around under the hall light, I could see that she had been crying.

"Lani, what in the devil is the matter?"

"I don't know!" It was almost a wail. She grabbed my hand again, and dragged us into the kitchen. She released me next to the chair where George had sat, so I parked and Maggie took my former chair. Lani went to the refrigerator and clinked a stream of ice into three glasses. She set those on the table, and went back for three cans of Coke before she sat down.

Both girls popped the tops on their cans and poured, but I couldn't help remembering William's liquor cabinet, and it seemed to me that I had seen a bottle of Myers dark rum in there. I wrestled with my good taste, lost to Myers' good taste, and walked over to grab the bottle. I splashed half an inch over the ice, and poured the Coke. I made a tentative offering gesture to both girls, got two head shakes, and took the bottle back to the liquor cabinet. You can't describe the flavor of Myers, or what it does for a Coke, but believe me, Coke is wasted without rum.

"Okay, Lani, take your time. Tell us exactly what you think is going on. By the way, where is your mother?"

"Mother went back to Las Vegas. I think she wants to move there, but I don't want to go. All of my friends are here."

I'd heard that before, approximately everytime that a family with teenagers decides to move.

Seemed like a good place to insert some social work. "Lani, it's hard to believe this now, but in a couple of years your best friends will drift away. In five years, you won't recognize them on the street, but your mother will always be your mother."

"Yeah, I know what you mean, Dick, but Regina isn't really my mother. She's my stepmother, and both of us are counting days until my eighteenth birthday."

"When did Regina leave?" I asked.

The Dealership

"Three days ago, just before the trouble started."

"And the trouble is …"

"Well, they said it's the missing Daewoo. See, they don't know when it disappeared because they closed up during the Merrie Monarch Festival. A few days after the festival, they noticed that the Daewoo was gone and called the police. Hal, the detective, said that it was an inside job because the keys were left in a key locker, and they were missing.

"He did talk to a taxi driver who took a couple of criminal types out to the lot during the festival, and another one who took the same guys to the airport, but Hal doesn't think they were the car thieves. Anyway, two of the salesmen decided that Daddy must have taken it. They came out and tromped all over the house and practically accused me of stealing it. They left, but they come back every night. I can hear them crashing around in the brush, late at night, and I'm scared silly. You guys will stay over? I should offer you some dinner."

"We'll stay." I decided. Maggie almost broke her neck nodding her affirmative.

"How about hamburger steaks and potato pancakes?" Lani jumped up and opened the refrigerator.

"I'll peel potatoes," Maggie offered.

I took my drink with me and went out to the living room to inspect William's gun rack. He didn't have a pistol, but he did have a Winchester .222 with a ten-cartridge-tube and it was loaded. It looked about right for marauding car salesmen in the night.

When I poked my head into the kitchen, it was starting to smell pretty good in there. Maggie had a pile of potatoes peeled, and was dicing an onion; Lani was frying garlic cloves in butter. "Lani, do you have a flashlight?"

"Sure." She wiped her hands on her apron, pulled a flashlight out of a drawer, and handed it to me. It was a good one, D cells and rubber coated, but I would have rather had the baseball bat variety, like the rookie cop had used to blind me in Sally's driveway.

Lani noticed that I was carrying her father's rifle. "Don't you guys carry guns?" she asked.

"Oh, sure, normally, but we came by airplane with no luggage. If Maggie and I had brought our guns, we'd still be in Honolulu filling out paperwork." I'm still trying to decipher the look that Maggie shot at me.

Chapter Twenty-Three

Lani went back to a cutting board and started molding hamburger patties. I took the flashlight and the rifle and stepped outside. I did remember to put the snap lock on the latch so I wouldn't lock myself out. Except for light from the windows, Mountain View was doing its dark trick again. I walked around the lanai. The end of the living room had no windows because of the fireplace on that wall, so no light came from there, but a nice swath spread out from the kitchen window that was over the sink. There appeared to be fifty feet around the house that was relatively clear, grass between shrubs and palm trees. That ended in a solid wall of jungle.

I walked around under the big window in the dining area. The lanai there was on stilts, the hill dropping down almost as steeply as the hill under Sally's windows. A door onto the lanai just past the kitchen would be the end of the main hallway, then several windows, probably bedrooms, but no lights were on in them. When I rounded the corner, heading back toward the front of the house, I snapped on the flashlight and got a healthy beam, but the lawn seemed to match the other side of the house—cleared for 50 feet, then jungle.

I went back inside and snapped the bolt again. I couldn't have stayed away from that kitchen if I had tried. The scintillating aroma sucked me in like the edge of a tornado. I put the rifle and the flashlight in the gun cabinet and followed my nose. I hadn't eaten since breakfast, and that seemed like a long time ago.

Maggie had set three places, and the center of the table was filling up with little bowls: kim chee, olives, pickles, cherry tomatoes, peppers, celery hearts, pickled okra, all of it gathered around a silver candlestick. The girls were chattering away, in English, I think, but the words or the subjects weren't registering. I took the right-hand chair so that the girls would be seated together. I felt just a little like a voyeur where I had no business being.

I was thinking about hitting the liquor cabinet again when Lani came over and set three wineglasses. Maggie set down a platter of hamburger patties and another of golden-brown latkes. Lani whipped off her apron, poured from a chilled bottle of Zinfandel, lit the candle, snapped off the light, and dinner was served.

That was one of the best meals I've ever eaten. If I could describe it, I'd give up detecting and write for *Gourmet Magazine*. The greatest thing about it was those two gorgeous young women chattering away in the candlelight. There was so much beauty, so much vitality, such spontaneity and enthusiasm. I was feeling like a dinosaur, but

I wasn't envying the guys, half my age, who would one day benefit from all of that. What I was doing was missing Betty with an almost physical pain. When life gets so good, when beauty approaches perfection, you need to share it, and I wanted to share this moment with Betty. I wondered what Maude and Betty were doing in Des Moines at that moment.

I noticed that the conversation had stopped and Lani was staring at me.

"Oh, don't worry about Dick." Maggie wrote me off with a dismissive wave. "He's thinking over the case and putting the clues together. Old detectives always do that." Maggie popped the last morsel of latke, covered with a quarter-inch of butter, into her mouth. I noticed that all our plates were empty and the table nearly bare.

Lani poured the last of the wine. "Let's leave the dishes, and build a fire." She carried her wine into the living room, knelt at the fireplace, and when she stood, the pleasant, spicy odor of burning kiawe wood wafted out, and the living room was lit by the flickering blaze. The girls settled down on the couch, still sipping wine. That was too much. I was in overload. I drained my wine, grabbed the rifle and the flashlight, and went back outside. *Betty, Betty, where are you when I need you?*

Gravel crunched while I walked down the lane. I inspected the gate with the flashlight. The bolt was half an inch thick, a steel cylinder in a solenoid. It was covered from the outside, so no one was going to move it with a penknife or a credit card. You could drive a car through it, and that's probably what had happened before our last visit, but no one was going to get in surreptitiously. I checked the fence on both sides of the gate. It ran into solid jungle within a few feet, so if the fence didn't continue, I didn't see why it would matter.

Grass around the edge of the jungle needed cutting, but that was a good thing. I was mashing down tracks when I walked on it, and no one else had walked there ahead of me. Up close, the jungle wasn't as solid as it had looked from a little distance. I tried walking into a gap that the flashlight showed, but in ten feet I was tangled in ivy, and the way was blocked by a spider web that you could play volley ball over. I found another spot that looked promising and followed the flashlight into what could have been a game trail. I made forty or fifty feet that time before I ran into a solid wall, but it wasn't a stroll in the park. I had the flashlight down trying to light a path, so I kept

Chapter Twenty-Three

getting slapped in the face with branches, and nearly strung myself up on a rope of ivy that hung across the trail.

After that, I settled for just shining the light into the jungle wherever it would go. At the back of the house, the ground dropped ten feet before the jungle sprouted up. If you jumped off that cliff, it wouldn't kill you but the brambles and thorns might make you wish that it had.

I walked back around the house and started at the cliff on the other side, but it was a repeat of what I'd already seen. It looked a highly unlikely place for car salesmen to be crashing around, and I couldn't imagine what Lani had been hearing. I wondered if she was just lonely and crying wolf, and I was glad that I had brought Maggie with me.

When I went back into the house, the fire was down to embers. The girls were in the kitchen, the table cleared, and the dishes washed and stacked in a drainer. A fresh bottle of Zinfandel stood on the table next to the candlestick, and they were sipping. An empty glass, apparently set for me, sparkled in the candlelight, so I wasn't totally forgotten.

Maggie looked up at me, did a double take, and bent over laughing. Lani's mouth and eyes popped wide open. She jumped up, but took a careful detour around me.

"The guest bathroom is in here," she said. I followed her, across the main hall, into another hall, and we made a right turn. She opened a door, turned on a light, and gestured me in. She wasn't talking anymore, because she was trying to suppress giggles. I stepped into the bathroom to see what all the mirth was about.

The guy in the mirror was a stranger, ninety years old, with gray hair, leaves and twigs sprouting out of him here and there. I ripped off my shirt, flapped most of the vegetation out of it into the bathtub. That only half worked, so I stripped and spent five minutes in the shower. It still took a while to comb the spider webs out of my hair. The image in the mirror was recognizable again, so I dressed and padded barefoot back to the bottle of wine. I'd noticed that there was quite a lot of dust in my throat that wasn't coming out.

"Jeez, Dick, what did you do? Fall into a garbage dump?" Maggie was having entirely too much fun at my expense.

"No, Detective Capriccio, I did not fall into a garbage dump. All I did was venture two feet off the lawn, and the jungle dumped on me." The wine wasn't chilled; it was cold, and it cleaned my throat right out. "Lani, I'm ready to believe in poltergeists. Whatever is crashing around out there can't be human."

Lani shuddered, and I was sorry for that crack, but I did conclude that she was not crying wolf.

"Just wait until you hear them," she said. "We may as well get some sleep. They don't come until early morning. You'll hear them when they come." She stopped and her gaze wavered back and forth between Maggie and me, not unlike the way that Noelani had looked at us at the airport. "Do you two share a room?" she asked.

I thought that was a diplomatic way of asking the question, but Maggie went into a fit of laughter that threatened to choke her. I certainly had no designs on Maggie; I'd be more apt to adopt her than take her to bed, but I really didn't see why the suggestion was so hilariously funny.

Lani betrayed me by laughing, too, so I guess there's something wrong with my sense of humor. I was surprised that we were retiring so early, but then I realized that the girls had drunk most of two bottles of wine and probably weren't used to that. I rescued them from further peril by emptying the bottle into my glass.

"Maggie, you can have Mother's room. I'll loan you some pajamas. Dick, you get the guest room at the front. It's the next door past the guest bathroom, and the noise comes from over that way, so you'll hear it first."

The bed was king-sized and solid, like the mattresses in Princeville. I shed shirt and socks, but stopped there. Lani hadn't offered me any pajamas, and under the circumstances, I felt funny about stripping. I flopped on top of the comforter, and must have blinked off myself when I shut off the light. After all, I had been up guarding the Chambers most of the previous night.

Chapter 24

I hadn't heard anything, but I sure felt it. Two young ladies in pajamas were bouncing on my bed and shaking my arms. They were talking to me, but in hushed tones, like they were afraid of being overheard, and most of what I got was: "Dick, Dick, wake up." I did that, and when I got my mind out of the stratosphere, the first thing I heard was an all-too-familiar hissing sound. You can make a noise like that by adjusting the nozzle on a garden hose for a spray and turning it onto a plate-glass window.

I was writing it off as just a tropical rainstorm, when I heard crashing brush and breaking sticks, even louder than the rain. That was one terrible moment, not because of the racket, but because Maggie and Lani obviously thought that I was going out in that rain to investigate.

That's a drawback of the macho image. You have to maintain it, especially when you have an audience, and it can get you into some miserable situations. I pulled my shirt on, skipped the socks, and turned the wrong way down the hall. Maggie pulled me back and steered me toward the front door. Lani ran to hand me the flashlight and the rifle. I scuffed my feet into my shoes, and the next thing I knew, I was shoved outside with the door closed behind me.

Strike that image of a fine spray; just turn the nozzle full blast, and point it straight down on your head. Water was running in a solid sheet off the roof. A gutter over the steps blocked the waterfall, but it didn't matter. The second I stepped off the porch, I was soaked right to the skin.

Even through the racket of the rain drumming on everything, including me, and the palm trees swishing around in the wind, I heard the crashing again, coming from the jungle on my left. It seemed to be closer to the road than it had been. I waded through Niagara to the edge of the jungle and tried to shine the light into the trees,

The Dealership

but all it did was light up a bubble of rain. However, the crashing was moving right along toward the road, and that was a good sign. I paced the noise that I had about decided must be a runaway elephant. I wondered if circuses ever came to Hilo?

The racket led me right down the drive to the gate, and past. I leaned the rifle against the gatepost, stuck the flashlight in my pocket, and climbed over. I was no longer expecting to meet Uzi-wielding salesmen. I shaded the flashlight lens with my fingers, pointed it straight down, and arrived at the road at the same time as the racket. I stepped out into the road and aimed the light at the noise, wondering if I should holler, "freeze."

It wasn't an elephant, but it was the biggest animal I have ever seen, at least up close in the dark in the rain. The beast that lumbered out of the jungle was a Brahma bull, and he was meeting my eyes without having to look up. We stood and stared at each other, twenty feet apart, water pouring off us like fountains. I'd been smelling that moldy odor that comes with rainstorms. Scientists claim that it's ozone; I think it's mold getting wet and waking up, but whatever, the smell of that wet bull steaming away overpowered it. I was wondering whether I could outrun this guy when it occurred to me that he might be blinded by the light. I snapped off the light. He stood there for one more minute; something that big you can see, even in total darkness. He snorted, turned away from me, and ambled off down the road. I would have started breathing again, but I might have drowned.

When I got back to the door, I was locked out, and it took quite a lot of pounding before an eye blocked the light from the peekhole. I shone the flashlight on my face.

"Is that you, Dick?" Lani shouted.

"Yes, that's me. Will you open the damn door?"

The door opened a crack, but not enough to step through. "Did you kill them?" Maggie asked.

"Oh, sure, they're dead and delivered to the morgue. Will you let me in?"

Lani pulled the door open. Maggie was standing in the hall with the shotgun. It took her several seconds to decide that the drowned rat standing there was really me, and lower the weapon. I made a mental note to check later and see if they had reloaded the shotgun.

I handed the rifle and the flashlight to Lani and bent to pull off my wet shoes. "Stay right there," she said, and ran down the hall. By the time I got the wet leather unstuck from my feet, she was back with a towel and a blanket. Maggie put the shotgun down and joined her.

Chapter Twenty-Four

Lani started on my head while Maggie peeled off my sodden shirt, and Lani wiped right on down to my belt line. She stopped there, and Maggie wrapped the blanket around my shoulders. I was allowed to walk down the hall, headed straight for the hot shower, leaving a creek behind me on the parquet that you could fish for trout in.

When I stopped shivering and climbed out of the shower, there was no way I was going to put on those wet pants and shorts. I wrapped myself in the blanket, and tried wringing out my pants, which didn't help much. I carried them next door to the bedroom, hung them over a chair, and crawled into the bed, starkers, to resume shivering. I made it just in time; Lani came in, collected my wet clothes, and slipped back out, holding them at arm's length.

I must have gone to sleep, because when I opened my eyes again, Maggie was sitting on the edge of the bed waving a cup of hot coffee under my nose. I noticed that she was dressed, so it must be morning, although it was still dark outside. Then I heard that hiss again, louder than it had been in the night. My clothes were clean, dry, and folded on a chair. Maggie handed me the coffee cup and slipped out.

Orange juice, more coffee, sausages, eggs, English muffins, and two gorgeous young ladies who thought I was the bravest man in the world. What more could you want for breakfast?

Lani knew all about the missing bull, and was glad I hadn't shot him because the owner who was looking for him had said he was worth eighteen thousand dollars. I was glad that I hadn't shot him, too.

We were sitting in our usual places at the table, but there wasn't any view. Outside, it was still dark; hard to believe it was eight-thirty in the morning. Water was coursing down the window in waves so it looked like frosted glass. I took my last cup of coffee out to the living room and cleaned and oiled the .222. That's the rifle that's known as a Hornet, with a muzzle velocity of over 3,000 feet per second, and I wasn't going to let that magnificent machine rust. The shotgun was not loaded, by the way.

Lani brought us each a 30-gallon garbage bag, and kissed our cheeks at the door, but did not step out. We held the bags over our heads, letting them stream out behind us, and ran for the car.

The wipers couldn't keep up. The lane looked wobbly, like an impressionist painting. I aimed for the center and stopped at the gate. Lani buzzed it open, and we made it to the road, but could not see across it. I reasoned that if there were traffic coming, it would be slow, and drove across until I could see the yellow line. I locked onto that, and we crept toward the highway.

Chapter 25

Wind tried to rip the car off the road. Water was running inches deep, sometimes with us, sometimes crosswise, and rain pounding on the metal roof threatened to deafen us. Most of the time, I could see the yellow line beside the car. When that stopped, Maggie reached into the back seat, grabbed her garbage bag, and bit a hole in it near the top. She crawled right into the bag until her eyes were behind the hole she had bitten, lowered her window and stuck her head out.

The sharp crack of rain on her garbage bag, added to the din on the car roof, was almost more than she could shout over. Rain was bouncing off her bag, pooling in the seat between us, and soaking me, but Maggie could see a white line on her side, scream directions, and we continued.

Eventually we broke out below the clouds, and visibility improved, but it still took us over an hour to make the last thirty miles into Hilo. We parked in front of the old building where Hal had his office. I held the plastic bag over my head and ran for the stairway, but Maggie had put hers on again, like a giant prophylactic, and strolled to the stairway with dignity.

Hal was in his usual sartorial splendor, green and brown motif again, leaning back in his swivel chair with his polished oxfords on the desk. He didn't actually wrinkle his nose, but conveyed his disapproval of our appearances.

"If that soggy specimen is the remains of Dick Payne, I'm amazed that you had the nerve to show your face in Hilo."

"Huh? How come?"

"Well, there are two taxi drivers ready to swear that you stole that car from the dealership, and they're watching for you around the clock."

It took me a second to realize that Hal wasn't talking about the Chrysler that George had stolen; he was referring to the missing

Chapter Twenty-Five

Daewoo. Maggie had taken a second to remove her bag and shake off the water. When she stepped through the door, Hal started that fishy-eyed glancing back and forth that I was getting used to.

"Hal," I said, "I'd like you to meet Detective Margaret Capriccio. She's an expert in criminal profiling, and we were lucky to hire her away from the Chicago Violent Crime detail." I figured he wasn't going to believe me anyway, so I laid it on thick. That way, if he believed just ten percent, he'd still be steered in the right direction.

"I'm happy to meet you, Detective Capriccio. I've been admiring your pictures."

"My what?"

"Your pictures. Spencer from the DEA was showing them around, not as a suspect, but someone to watch for. He said you've been island hopping using the alias, Sally Chambers. Your shorter hair looks much more modern, by the way."

"Little undercover job," I put in. "You know how it is." That was an unfortunate choice of words, but Hal let it go. He pulled some pictures out of his desk drawer, selected a few, and passed them over. "It seems there's a massive new supply of cocaine on the islands. Spencer is trying to track down the source, and everywhere he goes, Detective Capriccio is there ahead of him."

The pictures were of Maggie, lounging nearly nude by pools, dressed to the teeth and dining with various handsome hunks. I stopped and stared at the last picture, and leaned over to share it with Maggie. Hal noted the one I was staring at.

"That's just a bunch of tourists having breakfast in the Hanalei Room on Kauai." Spenser had snapped us at the moment that Maggie noticed him. She was leaning over, grabbing my arm, and I was struggling not to spill my pineapple juice.

I handed the pictures back to Hal. "Are you making any progress on the missing Daewoo?" I asked.

"Other than a couple of criminal types that the taxi drivers are watching for, no, but it apparently was an inside job. The keys were taken out of a locked office with no signs of a break-in."

"Did the two .38 slugs match?"

"Somewhere between maybe and probably. The one from Honolulu was pretty badly smashed by a very hard skull, but there's nothing about them that precludes a match."

"Would they stand up in court?"

"Nah, too vague, but unofficially I would say go for it."

The Dealership

Hal's phone rang. He put his feet on the floor, straightened his collar, and answered on the third ring. He listened a while, made a few grunts, then said, "Don't move," and hung up the phone.

"Come on. They just found the Daewoo washed up against a bridge pillar on the Hamakua Coast. There's raingear in the closet." Hal grabbed a slicker from the indicated closet. He slipped a pair of rubber galoshes over his immaculate oxfords and zipped. I grabbed the next slicker, but there weren't any more galoshes. Maggie was staring at her feet, which were shuffling a bit. Hal read her mind. "Oh, please join us, Detective Capriccio. You never know when we'll need a criminal profiled." He tossed a slicker to Maggie. The slickers were government issue, olive drab, meant to cover a man to his knees, and had a hood attached. Maggie struggled into hers, much happier to know that she was included, but the coat very nearly reached the floor, and I could see where her hands were, halfway down the sleeves. Hal locked up the office, we trooped downstairs, and climbed into his official SUV.

Hal cranked up siren and flashers. We crossed the bridge out of town, and in two minutes we were ripping along the Hawaii Belt Road. The SUV was higher than our rental, so we were looking down on the road at a better angle, more visibility. Hal was hitting fifty, but I figured the visibility justified twenty-five. The belt road runs along the coast, around the north side of 13,766-foot Mauna Kea. *Mauna Kea* means *white mountain*, so named because there is snow on top for half the year. At a hundred fifty feet taller than Mauna Loa, it is the tallest mountain in Hawaii, so when it comes within five miles of the coast, you get a spectacular coastline.

Hal slid to a stop on the shoulder behind a state trooper's blue-and-white, next to a concrete bridge. He ran up to talk to the trooper; I crossed the road and stared down into a canyon that looked about five hundred feet deep. It's not; it's less than three hundred feet, and the car was down there wedged against the bridge pier and looking very small.

The torrent I was looking down on is called The Kalekole Stream, and it's actually a tourist attraction because the Akaka Falls drop four hundred-twenty feet into it, just a couple of miles upstream. What I was looking down on did not look like a stream. It looked like a mill-race, and there sure weren't any tourists around. Hal came striding across the road, flipping up the hood of his slicker, and tightening the drawstring.

Chapter Twenty-Five

"The trooper checked, there's no one in the car, but we'd better have a look anyway." Hal walked past the end of the bridge, where I was clinging for dear life, and jumped off of what looked to me like a cliff. Did I tell you that macho images can be dangerous? I followed him over, wondering if I should holler, "Geronimo."

There were enough trees, bushes, and rocks that we weren't in free fall, but the slope was like the face of the average dam. We were going to make it to the bottom, along with a million gallons of water and acres of mud. I was wondering how we would get up again, and when I sneaked a look back, there was Maggie climbing down right behind us.

The pier that had snagged the car is not normally in the water, but the rain had changed that, and piled up a bunch of brush, besides. When we got to the river, it sounded like a freight train, even drowning out the water torture of rain on our hoods, and it smelled like moldy dead leaves. Water downstream from the car was only two feet deep, a kind of an eddy, and Hal splashed right into it. Water was pounding halfway up the doors on the upstream side, but was just below the downstream door. Hal jerked the back door open and looked inside.

I made it into the stream, unbelievably cold water to the knees, and peered over Hal's shoulder. "Not much damage, considering the plunge," I shouted.

"It didn't go in here. It went in upstream somewhere and washed down. Look, the key is still on and the transmission is in Drive." Hal was shouting, too; the noise level was like a rock concert. Sure enough, the key was in the ignition, a little chain with a tag swinging below it. Suddenly I knew why William Chun was killed.

"Hal," I shouted, "did you find William Chun's keys?"

"What keys?" Hal apparently thought the stress had driven me over the edge.

"His key ring, house keys, car keys, office keys. Were they in his pocket when you searched the body?"

Hal was looking upstream. His eyes popped wide open, then his mouth. "Run," he shouted. He was demonstrating how to do it.

I turned to follow him, one does not argue with a cop, but while I was turning around, I did notice that the linings were missing from the Daewoo's doors. I made it to the edge of the millrace, but Hal was scooting right on up. We met Maggie ten feet from the water, still working her way down. Hal grabbed one of her arms, so I

The Dealership

grabbed the other, and we dragged her backward up the bank. When Hal stopped, I looked back to see what all the fuss was about.

A wall of water, like a north-shore wave, was racing down that river, carrying enough logs on its crest to build a cabin. When it hit the bridge pier I felt the ground shake, and when I opened my eyes again, the Daewoo was gone.

It took thirty minutes to work our way back up that mudslide. Maggie was having some problems, but not because she wasn't physical enough; it was because her coat was too long. Hal and I were grabbing trees and rocks with both hands, but Maggie needed one hand to hold up the front of her coat. When she did step on the coat, she got a ten-foot-toboggan ride back down. Halfway up, she stopped being independent and let Hal and me pull, push, or pass her from hand to hand, as appropriate.

We muddied Hal's SUV, and when we got out back at the station, Maggie and I both stood in the gutter. A foot of water was racing along, and it cleaned the mud off our shoes. Hal, of course, just slipped off his galoshes and marched up the stairs. He was wet to the knees, but remarkably un-muddied.

Maggie and I stood just inside the door, dripping a puddle on the old brown linoleum. Hal sat down in his chair to do his dripping, but did not put his feet up.

"Now, what was that you were asking about keys?"

"I asked if you had found any in his pockets."

Hal went to a filing cabinet and pulled out a folder. "No keys," he decided. "This is a list of what he did have, not what he didn't have, but you're right. Everyone carries a few keys in their pockets. So, we finally have a motive for Chun's murder; he was killed for his keys."

"Yeah." I didn't want Hal taking all of the credit for my insight, so I plowed ahead. "Someone wanted that car badly enough to kill for it, and wanted the theft unnoticed for a while, but when they got the car, they pushed it into the creek. Did you notice what was missing from inside the car?"

"You mean the door liners all ripped off? Hey, Detective, do you suppose there were cookies from grandma hidden inside those doors?"

We ran the car heater full blast, all the way back to the airport, and were no wetter than a Seattle winter when we queued up at the departure gate. I dropped Maggie off at her apartment, and picked

Chapter Twenty-Five

up the mail, mine and Maude's. Maude's orchids were still alive, so I gave them a glass of water each, and closed her windows in case the Hilo rainstorm followed us to Oahu. I dragged myself home, wrapped a blanket around my shoulders, and treated myself to a healthy cocktail of vitamin C salts.

Chapter 26

Maggie had a new box of tissues on her desk, but she wasn't sniffling; she looked radiant. "Good morning, Dick. Sleep well?"

"Sleep? I died. How did you make out?"

"Wonderful. I did my aerobics and went right to sleep. Wasn't that the most scrumptious trip?"

"Marvey-fab. Is someone in our office?" I'd noticed that the light was on in there and I usually turn it on myself.

"George was already here when I came in. I made some coffee; can I bring you a cup? I told George how you solved the mystery of the missing Daewoo."

"I'll get the coffee. Thanks, Maggie." George was attached to the computer, just like I had left him—could that have been only two days ago? I grabbed a cup, drizzled it full, and plunked down at my desk. George was doing a printout, maybe his Christmas list.

"Is that the list of murderers?" I asked. The coffee was good, definitely better than the pot I had made at home.

George stacked up his pages. "The murderer is on this list."

"Are we going to throw darts at it to pick him out?"

"We're not, but Sally is. Are you ready to go to work, or are you going to drink coffee all day?"

I gulped the last half cup and followed George to the elevator. "Did you make some brilliant breakthrough while I was risking my life in a catastrophic deluge?"

"No, but you did. Maggie tells me that you brilliantly deduced that the missing car was packed with cocaine or heroin. That's the motive for both murders, and I suspect it's a regular pipeline for drugs. Darren must have threatened to interrupt the flow, and someone thinks that Sally might carry through his plan."

Chapter Twenty-Six

"You mean that Darren was dealing drugs?" I couldn't quite believe that. George had climbed into the passenger seat, so I drove the Jag.

"No, I just think that Darren threatened the operation, probably without ever realizing that it existed."

We made the turn through six lanes of rush-hour dregs onto Ala Moana Boulevard and headed for Kaimuki. "So, what is so special about your list?" I asked.

"This is a list of every employee who has ever seen or heard of a Daewoo."

"Not just Harry Kim? Surely he's confessed on the phone by now."

"Well, Harry is on the list, but that guy is so straight he's boring. Ever listen to a guy talking baby talk to his kids in Korean?"

"A pleasure I haven't had. Why cocaine or heroin? Why not pot?"

"Dick, sometimes you amaze me. Are you really that innocent? Hawaii doesn't import pot; Hawaii exports it. Surely you've heard of Maui Wowie, and you must know why Kauai is called the Garden Island. Sheesh, we're living in the pot capital of the world. You do know the Hawaiian word, *pacalolo*?"

"I thought the Feds were stamping it out, helicopter sprayers and such." We left the freeway and started up Wilhemina Rise.

"Well, sure they're working on it. Political pressure from California—we were threatening California's economy."

I paused at the entrance to Chamber's drive. "Sally is expecting us?"

"Yep, blink your lights a couple of times."

I blinked the headlights. Hiro stepped out of the alarm-room door and waved us in. He had exchanged the white sling that the hospital had given him for a dark blue one that matched his uniform. No alarms went off. Hiro waited by the door until we got out of the car, then he walked over and handed me the Beretta, butt first. I raised my eyebrows. He used his left hand, sling and all, to flip his jacket open. He had a new .357 snuggled in his shoulder holster, and he patted it with a very self-confident smile.

Sally was wearing that black jumpsuit again, the one that I think is called hostess pajamas. Her hair was positively shining, and she must have been wearing makeup. Not that I could detect it, but no woman could look so perfect without it. The maid ushered us into Sally's sitting room and served tea there. I guess none of us wanted to try the patio.

"Hi, George. Hi, Dick. Lani tells me that you go in for bull fighting in the rain." Sally extended a hand, but we didn't exactly shake it, we each sort of held hands with her for a moment.

George ushered Sally into a big overstuffed chair and plunked himself down on the couch next to me. This was his show, so he was lecturing.

"Sally, remember we discussed motive, opportunity, and means to solve a crime?"

Sally nodded and settled down into the chair with her tea in her hand.

George continued. "The means were obvious, and now we have the motive, or at least the prime mover behind the motive, but there is something wrong, and it must be with opportunity. I have here a list of names, and most of them have been eliminated, but we must have missed something. What I need you to do is relax and free associate. I'll read a name. You just say the first word that pops into your head. Ready?"

Sally leaned forward to set her tea on the coffee table, then leaned back, crossed her knees, and closed her eyes. She nodded. George started down the list.

There were a few that Sally responded "nothing," but mostly she gave George a word and he wrote it down. They were things like hustler, flirt, boring, young, but none that sounded helpful to me. When George read Harry Kim, she said Teddy Bear. Ronald Murphy was golf. I thought we were wasting time until George read Willis Lee and Sally said: "fired."

George and I shouted, "What?" together. Sally opened her eyes and sat up, shaking her head like she needed to wake up. George and I were remembering that Willis Lee was the Daewoo salesman who was having his fortune told by Madam Zenobia at the time William Chun was murdered. Obviously he hadn't had the opportunity, but according to the company files that we had gone over, Willis was very much still on the payroll.

"Why did you say fired?" George asked.

"Well, maybe not fired, but Darren was planning to have a talk with him. I thought Darren was going to fire him."

"Why?" George asked. "He's one of your top salesmen."

"Yes, he is, but he was spending too much time off island, and Darren was expecting trouble."

"Off island? You mean he was missing too much work?"

"Not exactly that. You see, the salesmen can name their own hours. They almost work for themselves. We pay them the minimum wage to keep legal, but their income is from commissions, so whether they work or not is up to them. Darren was worried because Willis was spending too much time in Las Vegas."

Chapter Twenty-Six

"And that's cause for firing?" George had been shaking his head for a while.

"It means trouble down the road. It's like if a guy is drinking too much, or maybe taking drugs, and he may be functioning just fine, but you know there will be trouble in the future. Darren tried to steer clear of future problems, so he wanted to get Willis away from gambling before Willis got into debt and was tempted to try something desperate."

"Something desperate, like?"

"Like anything, whatever. For instance, we had a salesman sell a car for cash and neglect to mention the sale. The car wasn't missed for months, stuff like that."

George stood up and folded his list.

"Is that all the names?" Sally asked.

"No, and we may be back, but it's time for Dick to get his fortune told." George was already headed for the door. I gave Sally the bewildered shrug that I felt, and followed George.

I headed the Jag down Wilhemina Rise. After the trip down into the canyon the day before, Wilhemina Rise didn't seem so steep. "Why am I getting my fortune told? Why not you? Your future is pretty shaky."

"I'd love to," George was reading his list again, but had his finger on Willis. "Only I've got to get back to the computer. Won't this dog go any faster?"

"What's so important about the computer? Were you winning a game of solitaire?"

"I always win solitaire, but this time I'm into the numbers racket. There was one of those coincidences that never happen with that stolen Daewoo."

"And that would be?"

"The serial number ended in double zeros."

"So?"

"So, no matter how long and complicated the serial numbers may get, every one-hundredth is going to end in double zeros. You could say that that particular car was one in a hundred. I want to trace the last few double zero sales. Now that you're spending half your nights with Maggie, you need your future told, if you have a future."

George had a good idea there; he just didn't know it. I wasn't getting my fortune told, but Maggie was, and if I went along, this time it would be as her father.

Chapter 27

Maggie called Madam Zenobia and had no problem making an appointment for seven that evening. "It's going to cost fifty dollars, is that okay?"

I opened her desk drawer and handed her two twenties and two tens from the cash box. "If she tells you good things, tip her. I'm going with you, by the way. You can introduce me as your father."

"Gee, I don't know, Dick." Her face screwed into a frown, somewhere between worried and alarmed. "Madam Zenobia sees all, knows all, and tells all. I mean, it might be sort of embarrassing."

"Don't worry about it. If it's sex you're thinking of, I probably wouldn't understand it anyway."

She nodded, and looked relieved. I think she believed me. "I'll pick you up at your place at six forty-five. Why don't you take off early and get prepared?"

"Good idea." I didn't have to argue, Maggie was already skipping out the door.

George came bounding out of the office, holding another printout, and I think he was kissing it. "Bingo, gotcha, all that good stuff. Willis Lee has personally sold the last three double-zeros, and get this. The first and the third sales were for cash."

I felt the tension drain out of my body. It's funny, when you're on a case you don't feel tense, but when a breakthrough comes, you feel tension go away anyhow. "Terrific, can we arrest him?"

"What for, selling cars?"

"Shall we tail him?"

"No, there's a new shipment coming in tomorrow. We're going to tail the one-hundredth car. You just figure out how he was in two places at once."

Chapter Twenty-Seven

The phone rang. I reached across Maggie's desk and grabbed it: "Payne and Clark."

"Hi, Dick, did you water my orchids?"

"Yep, they were hale and hearty last night, and they told me they miss you."

"That's a good boy. I'll be home tonight at eight-thirty. Pick me up by the United baggage carousel."

"Maude, I might be a little late, I have an appointment ..." I was talking to a dead telephone. Maude still considered telephones newfangled, and hadn't much use for phone etiquette. She'd said what she had to say, so she hung up the phone. No problem, really. I'd pick Maggie up at six forty-five, get her fortune told at seven, drop her off at seven forty-five and be at the airport at eight-thirty.

I stopped in front of Maggie's house at six forty-four. It's on Date Street in an area of ancient, single-family houses and new rectangular cinderblock duplexes, all of it slowly sinking into the ground. I did have a momentary conscience attack, thinking maybe we should give her a raise, but managed to stifle it.

Maggie came swirling out the door the moment I stopped. I knew it was her by the place and the time. I suspect that the outfit had been purchased on Maui by Mrs. Sally Chambers. Red heels, sheer hose, red dress, with practically no top because all of the material had been used up making the skirt. The top was going to stay up, because it was hooked on a pair of designer nipples. The skirt was short, very short, but there were yards of pleats and swirls. Her purse matched her shoes, and she held it under her arm, secured by a white-gloved hand. My instincts did a flip, back to high school, and I rushed around the car to hold the door for her.

Madam Zenobia's lair is on Keeaumoku Street, one block from the Ala Moana shopping mall, which is the busiest area in Waikiki. That could have been a problem, but at six fifty-five, business was slow at the Sam Sung Plaza, so I parked in a *customers only* spot. We trooped up the stairs, past the music store, and jangled the bell over Madam Zenobia's door at seven.

We stepped into a waiting room; no Madam Zenobia. What was there was a purple couch, period. The walls were covered by fuzzy drapes, velvet, I think, that matched the couch. The light was a crystal chandelier with a jillion hanging prisms, but the bulbs were tiny, like for a Christmas tree; all of them red. Air currents from the closing door had set the prisms to swinging, so there were little red spots flitting around the room, like a hundred Tinkerbells. It was the sort of room where you do not talk, so Maggie and I perched on the couch, scuffed our feet in the purple carpet, and tried not to get dizzy from the lights.

I figured out that two of the drapes on the wall opposite our couch were actually a doorway. The clue was the shrieks and heart-wrenching sobs that were coming through them. When I listened hard, I could hear a low, steady voice droning in the background, like a hypnotist putting someone to sleep, but it didn't seem to be working; the sobbing was sliding up and down the scale like a police siren.

Maggie's eyes were open wide. She hadn't looked scared when we were shot at on Kauai, nor while she held the shotgun on the soggy intruder in the night. Not even when we were in danger of drowning in a mudslide, but she was scared now. It was like waiting in a dentist's office when a screamer is in the chair.

The sobbing stopped with a choke and a cough. A great sigh wafted out, followed by: "Oh, thank God." Then hand clapping, and "Oh, thank you, thank you, Madam." A moment later the curtains parted and two women stepped into the room. The fortyish executive in the sharp business suit was smiling, but wiping her eyes with her handkerchief. The one who was a hundred years old wore a turban and a cloak, made from some leftover drapery. The executive ducked past us and escaped, the illusion-in-purple advanced on us.

"Miss Capriccio?"

Maggie nodded. The apparition turned to me. "And you are?"

"Mr. Capriccio. My little girl is getting married next month and she's nervous. You were highly recommended as the one who could calm her fears."

That brought a smile, perfect teeth, made in a jewelry store. The eyes were not smiling; they were piercing, and they were at least fifty years younger than the rest of her. "That's nice to hear. May I ask who recommended me?"

"Oh, just a guy I work with. I'm with the Chambers Auto Group and one of our salesmen mentioned you. Willis Lee?"

She frowned at the name, and she wasn't making a connection.

"Yeah, Willis seemed to think that you're the greatest. He happened to mention that you take American Express, and he used his company card ..." Still no flash of recognition. "The Chambers Auto

Chapter Twenty-Seven

Group, executive American Express Card?" I had started to wonder if Madam Zenobia really knows all, when she gave me that mouth-only smile again.

"Oh, of course, Lee, but you misunderstood. It isn't Willis who comes in; it's his wife, Lois. In fact, she was in just a week or so ago. Lovely lady, but so terribly worried. I do hope that all is well with Willis." It was her turn to pump me, and anything I told her would come in handy during her next session with Lois.

"Oh, everything is fine. Willis is the best salesman we have. You know, I've never met his wife. What is she like anyway?"

"She's a very attractive lady, tall and slender type. She has long, red hair like a goddess, but, you know, I'm worried about her. I see gambling in her cards."

Madam was still playing the information game, and I was happy to play with her. I'd bet a lot that she had seen a ticket to Las Vegas in Lois's purse.

"Well, Willis does make the occasional trip to Las Vegas, but I wouldn't worry; he makes plenty of money at the dealership." I glanced at my watch, seven-twenty, not good. "I appreciate your taking care of my little girl here." I patted Maggie's bare shoulder. "You go right ahead and get your fears calmed down, sweetheart. I'll wait for you in the car."

Madam turned to lead the way through the curtains, Maggie right behind her. "And hurry," I hissed at Maggie.

It was five after eight when Maggie came floating down the stairs. I'd never encountered rapture before, but Maggie was in it. I closed her door and jumped into the car to peel out of the parking lot. Maggie didn't even notice when I crossed Beretania, headed for the freeway and the airport instead of her apartment.

"Oh, Dick, it's going to be wonderful. Dashiell and I are going to have four kids, two boys and two girls, and get very rich. The kids will all become professionals, and Dash and I will live out our happy old age in the Bahamas."

"Who the hell is Dashiell?" I asked. We were merging with the freeway.

"He's the handsome hero in the book I'm reading. Hey, where are we going?"

"Airport. I'm supposed to pick up my eighty-year-old neighbor in about ten minutes." I wheeled into the parking lot with five minutes to spare, and used them all looking for a spot. We took the

147

The Dealership

elevator down to the arrival area. I was walking fast, and Maggie held my arm to keep up. I spotted Maude, standing with her back to me, suitcase in hand. I recognized her by her coat, and the little blue hat with the veil and the gnats on it. I walked up behind her and took her suitcase.

"Oh, hi, Dick, you're late. I have a surprise for you."

Surprised, shocked, overwhelmed, sucker-punched in the solar plexus. The redhead standing behind Maude was Betty, and all I could do was stare. Betty was staring too, but she wasn't looking at me. She was looking at Maggie.

"Surprised, Dick? So am I. I'll get the next plane back to Des Moines." Betty was backing away from me. I dropped the suitcase and charged.

"No, you won't." I grabbed her in a bear hug, and squeezed the breath out of her, just like in my dream. "Betty, you are never leaving me again. I want my arms around you for the rest of my life, and if you can't stand it here, then I'm going to Des Moines with you." I noticed that Betty looked blurry, and that was because there were tears in my eyes. The hell with macho.

Betty was looking at me now, and at least hesitating, if not thawing. "Who is your new friend?"

I kept a firm grip on Betty with one hand, just in case, but motioned to Maggie with the other. "Betty, this is Maggie Capriccio, our secretary. She did a special assignment for us tonight, that's why the glad rags, and that's why I'm late.

"Maggie, this is Betty, my fiancée. We're the ones who are going to get married, have the four professional kids, get rich, and live out our happy old ages together in the Bahamas. Come on, let's get out of here, we have catching up to do." I picked up both suitcases, but I had Betty's hand captured under my arm, and I wasn't letting go. "Maude, Maggie, my secretary. Maggie, Maude is the best neighbor that anyone ever had."

We wheeled up in front of Maggie's apartment. Maggie and Maude were in back, I still hadn't let go of Betty's hand.

Maggie leaned in the passenger window. "Betty, I'm really glad to find out that Dick has a girlfriend. I can't imagine how such a dork ever caught you, but I'm glad that he did. Dick, are you coming to work tomorrow?"

"Maybe. If you don't see me for a couple of weeks, tell George that Willis's alibi is shot to hell—oh, and tell him all about Lois Lee. In

Chapter Twenty-Seven

fact, call Sally and get a description of Lani's mother, I have a feeling that this Las Vegas business is another non-existent coincidence."

"I don't need to call Sally. I saw a picture of Lani's mother, and Madam Zenobia was describing her. Have fun." Maggie swirled away.

I set the two suitcases inside Maude's door, but I kept hold of Betty's hand. Maude ran to the refrigerator, pulled a bottle of Corbel Brut and two glasses out of the chiller, and handed them to Betty. "Good night, dears," she said.

Chapter 28

I did go in to work, but it was close to nine-thirty. Betty had an appointment to get her old job back, and needed to do some unpacking. Sure, we did what you're thinking, and if I kept score, you'd think I was bragging; but mostly we talked all night, chattering away like a couple of mynah birds.

Maggie gave me a conspiratorial wink. There was no doubt what she thought we'd been doing, and she probably thought that I'd learned about sex last night. George was watching the numbers on his watch march by, like I did while I was waiting for Maggie at Madam Zenobia's.

"Just in time, Dick. The barge has docked and the cars will be unloading momentarily. The cars were loaded frontward but will come off backward, so the one hundredth will be the first one off. It's bright red, consigned to a lot in Wahiawa, but it would be good to watch it all the way. You pick it up at the dock on Sand Island and follow it until the truck turns on H-2. I'll take over there. By the way, I figured the convertible would be too conspicuous, so I rented a Ferrari hard-top."

I had picked up a cup and headed for the coffee pot, but George was nixing that. "Better get going. We don't want any snafus from tailing the wrong car."

Cars were coming off the barge fast, looking like toys dangling from those giant cranes. Trucks were lined up two deep, all the way down the dock, but the first truck in line was still being loaded, and I hadn't missed any because I would have met them on Sand Island Road. The first car on the truck, bottom tier, front, was a red sedan. "Payne and Clark always get their car" is our motto.

The truck turned left on Nimitz Highway and climbed up onto the H-1 Freeway. I followed a block behind, past Pearl City and

Chapter Twenty-Eight

Waipahu. We were coming down the hill toward the junction with H-2 when a lemon-yellow Ferrari flashed past and cut in front of me. George was hunched over the wheel. I dropped back, but turned onto H-2. I love it when something goes according to plan.

At the end of the freeway, I pulled up behind George. The truck turned left at the bottom of the ramp. George continued straight ahead, and I followed the truck to the car lot. We were in that section of untamed wilderness outside Wahiawa—no sidewalks. I parked on the shoulder where I could watch the truck through a suitable screen of bamboo. George came strolling through the grass behind me and kicked my door. I had to open it for him because he had a Styrofoam cup of coffee in each hand.

George bent down to hand me a cup and climbed in, trying not to spill his own coffee. It was scalding hot, but not from McDonalds, so there was no warning label on it.

"Now what?" I asked.

"Now, we never take our eyes off that car until someone buys it. That's why I brought you coffee; it may be a long shift. You do have an empty jug with you?"

"Yeah, it's in the trunk." Detective course 101, lesson two: Always keep an empty jug handy, because you can't leave your post just because your bladder is about to burst. George handed me a folded sheet of paper. It was a computer printout, a blowup of a Hawaii State driver's license. The picture was of a big, athletic-looking guy, smooth shave, lots of curly black hair, and a smile so sincere that you wanted to buy a car from him. The vital statistics were 6 foot, 190 pounds, Willis Lee.

"Where did you get that?"

"Off the Hawaii State computer system. Want a copy of yours?"

I should have noticed that George was slurping down his coffee too fast. I had barely started mine when he opened the car door and climbed out. He was looking at his watch. "I'll relieve you, shall we say six until midnight?" I looked at my watch. It was seven hours until six, but when I looked up again, George was gone.

George was right, it was a long shift, and so was the one from midnight until six in the morning. I spotted Willis Lee pretty soon. He was out there selling cars, but never went near the red Daewoo. I have a copy of Dostoevsky's *The Idiot* that I've been reading on stakeouts for years. I never bother to mark my place, because it doesn't matter where you are in the book, nothing is happening anyway, but you stay wide-awake. The car lot was closed when I relieved George at midnight. He didn't wait to talk to me, just drove away when I pulled up behind him. He parked behind me again at six in the morning. I drove home, the car lot was still closed, and the red Daewoo was still in place.

I scrambled eggs with Spam—that's the traditional Hawaiian breakfast—and wolfed them down. Betty came over from Maude's at seven, dressed for work, heels and hose for the lawyer's office.

"Good morning, Dork."

"Good morning, Girlfriend."

We latched into a hug and I swung her around while we kissed. When I set her down again, she was out the door and I collapsed on the bed, daring my alarm clock to try to wake me at eleven-thirty. That was no problem because Maggie called me while the alarm was still ringing, just to be sure that I was up. I did check to see that my cell phone was charged, and stuck it in my pocket.

Willis Lee was having a good day. He showed several cars, shook lots of hands, clapped several backs, and some of the cars drove away. By ten minutes before six, I was thinking mostly about some supper. It seemed like I should take both Betty and Maude out, and I was wondering if we could get a table at Duke's. Because it's located right on Waikiki Beach, Duke's is the place to take tourists. Duke was an Olympic champion swimmer, practically invented the surfboard, and was in a lot of movies back in the thirties. Tourists love the place and the pictures. Betty wasn't really a tourist, but she'd been away for a while, so she almost qualified.

Willis came out of the showroom again, and I very nearly crawled under the dashboard. He had two guys with him, and unless Cy had more brothers, one of them was the assassin who had shot at us on Kauai. The three of them walked back to the red Daewoo, and Willis was giving them a sales pitch, apparently with success. The red sedan was blocked by other cars, but a couple of lot boys came out and started jockeying a path. George drove up behind me, but he saw what was happening and drove on down the road. In a couple of minutes, I saw him park two blocks ahead on the opposite side, headed back toward me.

Detective school 101, lesson 3: Whichever way your car is pointing, your quarry will go the other way. It did. The Daewoo pulled out of the lot, a different guy driving, and my assassin riding shotgun, as it were. They turned toward me. I buried my nose in my book, and

Chapter Twenty-Eight

George came by half a block behind them, being inconspicuous in that yellow Ferrari.

I let them disappear around the corner before I pulled a U-turn and burned rubber after them. They had two choices: they could either get back on the freeway, or go through town. At decision time, I didn't see the Daewoo, but that yellow Ferrari was stuck at a stoplight at the entrance to Schofield Barracks. You remember Schofield from the accounts of the attack on Pearl Harbor, and that base is probably why the town of Wahiawa exists.

If they were leaving town, they would probably head for the Kamehameha Highway, but that involved a couple of major intersections. At the first intersection, the Daewoo turned, George went straight, and I followed the Daewoo. At the next intersection, George cut in front of me again and I pulled off. That got us onto the Kamehameha and I hung back, letting George keep them in sight. Once you're on a main artery, they wouldn't expect you to turn off, and if they spotted the yellow Ferrari, they would know that no one would use such a monstrosity to tail them.

The Kamehameha Highway leads across the belly of Oahu, past the Dole pineapple plantation and through the coffee fields. When you start down the hill, you start getting glimpses of the ocean again, this time across the island from Honolulu. George was keeping several cars behind the Daewoo, which is fine on the highway, but dangerous in town. I passed some cars where I shouldn't have, and passed George just as we got to the traffic circle where you decide between the towns of Haleiwa, Mokuleia, or continue on toward Waimea and the North Shore. The Daewoo turned toward Haleiwa, with me three cars behind them.

Haleiwa is a funky old town, but a nice one. Mostly it's art galleries and restaurants, and has a great marina. By the way, in Hawaii the letter "W" is pronounced like an English "V." A native will tell you that he's from "Ha-*va*'-ee," so Haleiwa is pronounced like holly in a Christmas wreath, and Eva like in Peròn. Break Eva into two syllables with the accent on the first, and pronounce "holly-*eev*'-ah" like a native.

We turned left just before the bridge, headed toward the marina and the road that curves left again and follows the beach. We were the only two cars that turned, so I pulled into the parking lot at the marina. From there, I could see down the coast road for several blocks. I felt pretty safe because most of the roads that turn off in-

The Dealership

land again are one-block-long dead ends. If the Daewoo took a road that went clear through, back to the main highway, they would be completing a circle. That would mean they had spotted the tail and we had blown it.

The Daewoo went down two blocks and turned left. I screeched out of the parking lot and raced past the road where they had turned, just as they pulled into a clapboard garage halfway down the block. I went right on by and was leaning against the Jag, enjoying the salt spray from the surf, when George pulled up behind me.

The area is old, large lots and small houses, with trees on every lot. A few homes had papaya and banana groves, others just had whatever grew there to begin with. The north side of the road is bordered by a grass verge with palm trees scattered and surf pounding the beach thirty yards away. On the north side of the island, the trade winds are on-shore, hence the sobriquet, "Windward Side." They boost the ocean spray right across the road.

George had a little trouble extracting himself from the Ferrari, so his walk had a mechanical creak to it. The cramped quarters hadn't improved his mood.

"What, did you lose them in this confusing metropolis?"

"Nope, they're in a garage a couple of blocks back. Why don't you go ask them to come out? The last time I faced those guys, they singed my whiskers with a Kalashnikov."

"Maybe this would be a good time to call your old buddy, Lieutenant Cochran?"

"Call Cochran? Maybe I'd rather face the Kalashnikovs." But I dialed the precinct on my cell phone. Perfect timing. It was just seven, Cochran had been headed out the door, probably for a convention of warlocks, and had to come back in to take the call.

"Payne, this had better be very, very good. We found Chambers' car at the airport, washed on the way there, the inside swabbed down with alcohol, and not a fingerprint even near it."

"Did you check the seat cushions for business cards—wait, don't hang up. You're going to love this one. We have at least two murderers trapped in a garage, and you can tell Spencer that we found the spigot on his drug pipeline."

"Where the hell are you?" Cochran growled.

Chapter 29

It got dark, and the wind was blowing ocean spray over us. We'd turned the Jag around and were waiting in it with the heater running and using the windshield washers when the salt spray got too thick. The best thing that happened was that Willis Lee's Cadillac came gliding down the street and turned toward the garage. Wouldn't you know that a Daewoo salesman would drive a Cadillac?

We were parked two blocks from the turn off, but we had a good view and there was a streetlight on the corner, so no one was going to leave without our seeing them. We even had rule three covered. The Ferrari was across the street pointed in the other direction.

Cochran's unmarked blue Plymouth came slipping down the street and parked behind the Ferrari. I got out and walked across the road.

"So, where the hell is this desperate gang of cutthroats?"

"Second street behind you, halfway down the block on the left, unpainted clapboard garage."

"Why didn't you just arrest them? You are still a citizen, aren't you?"

"These guys don't like me. They keep shooting at me. Maybe they'll like you better."

"Probably. Most people do."

An identical blue Plymouth stopped behind Cochran, and Spencer from DEA joined us. Blue-and-whites were appearing from both directions and lining the street, all very quiet. I filled Cochran and Spencer in on the way the drug pipeline worked and gave them Willis Lee's name.

We looked like an army platoon marching down the road and turning onto the side street. There seemed to be a lot of guns around, rifles as well as service revolvers. When we got to the garage, it was dark, and Lee's car wasn't on the street, so I figured that both cars

The Dealership

were in the garage. Cochran stopped his platoon with a raised hand and did a lot of pointing and gesturing. Cops peeled off and slipped around the sides of the garage.

Cochran raised a bullhorn and awakened the neighborhood.

"This is the police. You are surrounded. Lay down your weapons and come out with your hands up."

Every one of the cops turned on one of those ten thousand-watt flashlights, and the garage looked like high noon. The garage doors wiggled. A dozen rifle bolts clicked. The doors swung open, and there stood four cops blinking in the light. With the door open, that garage looked like one of those covered bridges in New England. There wasn't any back, just a dirt lane leading off through the trees.

Flashlights were already swinging back down the lane out of the woods. It was only fifty yards to where the lane came out on another street, that one leading back to the highway.

When Cochran and Spencer got through swearing at us, and the blue-and-whites had departed, Cochran did condescend to take down the name Regina Chun, the alias Lois Lee, and a general description of Lani's mother. When I told him she'd probably be in Las Vegas, he said: "Okay, we'll stake out the Philippines," and drove away.

"Meet you at Fat Fat," George said. He climbed into the Ferrari.

George and I drove through the garage and the track through the woods. It was the fastest way back to the highway. I remembered to call Betty when we got to the highway. She wasn't particularly pleased, because Maude was planning piroshki for dinner and had the wine chilling. I bought her off by suggesting that she make reservations at Duke's for seven the next night.

Fat Fat in the evening was a different scene from our usual afternoon stops. Cy mixed our drinks while we worked our way past the booths. That was tricky because the booths were full and several of the groups took up more than one table, so conversations, as well as drinks and pupus, were crossing the aisles. Three stools were empty at the far end of the bar, one of them stable, the other two rejects. George grabbed the stable one and asked the sixty-four-thousand-dollar question.

"Did they go through the garage because they had spotted a tail, or was that part of their normal precautions?"

"The difference being?"

"If they know we're onto them, they'll be scrambling to get off the island, probably in a chartered submarine. The only good part is that they have no more excuse to kill Sally. If they didn't spot your clumsy

Chapter Twenty-Nine

tailing, they'll be doing business as usual, and Lee may even come to work tomorrow."

"In other words, if we assume they're all colorblind, and didn't notice your yellow Easter egg parked in the bushes, they'll be unpacking the car and drinking champagne?"

"Exactly, but if they noticed that you were holding that idiotic book upside down, they'll be off the island without a trace in the next couple of hours."

"Naturally you noticed that Lee's address is on his driver's license?"

"Naturally. It's an apartment, and he hasn't lived there for years. I checked it out yesterday while you were sleeping at your post."

We'd finished our drinks. Cy looked the question and we wavered. George made a *maybe later* gesture and laid a ten on the counter. Cy took the empties.

"Do you suppose that Sally might know where he lives? Chambers group seem to know their people pretty well."

"Worth a try." I pulled the modern social gaffe of using my cell phone in the bar.

"One moment please, I'll see if Mrs. Chambers is available."

"Tell her it's Dick Payne, and this is extremely urgent."

"Hi, Dick, where are you? Sounds like a party."

"That's the radio. Do you have any idea where Willis Lee actually lives?"

"His address is in the file ..."

"That's a phony. Does he have a beach house, or a hunting cabin, or a relative? We need to find him in the next couple of hours; everything depends on finding him fast."

Sally was thinking. Cy came around offering again, but George stalled him.

"Dick? Just maybe. About five years ago we had a company barbeque up in the mountains, and I had the impression that the place belonged to Willis."

"We'll check it. What's the address?"

"Heavens, I have no idea, if it even has an address, but I can find it. Meet us at Punaluu Beach Park."

I didn't like the sound of that, but Sally had hung up the phone. "Punaluu Beach Park," I said to George. He spun his stool around and headed for the door, missing Floralitta and her tray by inches.

"Leave that dog of yours. Let's go in a car for a change." George was climbing into the Ferrari, so I climbed into the passenger seat. It wasn't too bad, a lot more legroom than I had thought, once you

The Dealership

got used to the feeling of sitting right on the pavement. We were parked on Beretania. George bulled his way to Piikoi, jogged right, and climbed onto the freeway.

I was getting used to looking up under the trucks in the next lane when we screeched onto the Like Like Highway and thundered toward the mountains. The Like Like (Lee *kay* lee *kay*) climbs halfway up the Koolau Mountain Range, and takes the Wilson Tunnel right through it. You bust out of the tunnel and catch your breath, every time. You're looking down a thousand feet on a sea of lights that are the towns of Kaneohe and Kailua, and a jillion condos stretched along the Kamehameha Highway.

When you hit the highway, the lights taper off fast, and if George is driving, you're skirting the ocean on the right, mountains and jungle on the left, and leaving rubber on every curve, which is constantly. That ended when we came up behind a city bus and settled down to forty miles an hour for ten miles of no-passing zone.

Punaluu Beach Park isn't something you should look for. You've been driving past beaches, almost continuously, for miles. It's a park because there's fifty feet of space between the highway and the beach. When that happens, the state makes a turnout, puts up two tables and a barbeque, and gives the place a name.

We'd been sitting there for five minutes, not in the car, on it, when the limo slid into the parking lot. Hiro was driving, Sally beside him. George and I climbed in back, and Hiro pulled out, he had never actually stopped. We raced another half-mile along the beach, Sally pointed, and Hiro screeched onto a road that was marked *Tsunami Evacuation Road*.

We were on a paved road in a deep valley, but climbing fast. At the head of the valley, Sally pointed left, and after that I lost track; we were hopelessly lost in the mountains.

"Slow down, it's right around here somewhere, on the right-hand side." That wasn't very reassuring, but a driveway came up on the right with a wooden gate and *No Trespassing* signs. "That's it." Sally sat back and Hiro slid to a stop with the bumper almost against the gate. George and I piled out. The gate was locked with a padlock on a chain.

"Shall we shoot it off?" George asked.

"Too noisy."

"Who's going to hear it?" He had a point there. We were surrounded by mountains with no sign of civilization anywhere. I pulled the Beretta out of my pocket and shot the padlock right between the

Chapter Twenty-Nine

prongs of the bale. It made a tiny dent. "Wimp," George said, and blasted the lock with his Glock. That made another dent. Hiro trotted up behind us, pulled the .357 out of his holster, and *blam*, the padlock was gone, and so were a few links of the chain.

From there it was like that artillery song, "Over hill, over dale ..." and it was a dusty trail, usually completely covered by trees, occasionally breaking out to show the entire north coast of Oahu, then diving back into an arboreous tunnel. Eventually the trees thinned. Hiro snapped off the headlights and kept right on going by starlight.

When the trees ended, we were hanging on a shelf on the edge of a cliff, solid rock wall on the left, ugly black death on the right. The road was climbing, following the cliff like the scalloped lace on the edge of a doily, and Hiro was whipping us around those curves just as if he could see where we were going.

We topped the cliff, the rock wall on the left gave way to a field of broken lava, but the black jaws of death stayed with us on the right. We did have a wonderful view on the right, about thirty miles of highway five miles away and two thousand feet below us. Little towns were scattered along the highway, traffic busily connecting the dots, and the ocean making an amorphous sparkling horizon, but it was the view on the left that had our attention. A hundred yards of wild grass and lava rock led across the apron of the hill, and at the end of that were yard lights. Above the lights stood a mansion that would have looked like part of the hill if there hadn't been half an acre of glass reflecting the sky. Hiro stopped behind a lava outcropping and we silently eased out of the car.

I would have suggested that Sally wait in the car, but she was twenty yards ahead of us, scampering between the rocks. When we caught up with her, I saw that she had a .38 revolver in her hand. We stopped scampering and crept the last fifty yards. A big chunk of lava had grown right at the edge of a paved apron.

Lee's Cadillac was parked in a pool of light on the apron, and so was the Daewoo. Two guys were inside the Daewoo, handing out white plastic bags, and Lee was collecting them, standing with his arms full. George climbed up onto our rock, Glock extended, and shouted, "Freeze." They didn't freeze; they exploded. Two automatic rifles fired out of that car, and chips of lava were flying around us like hornets. George had already jumped off the rock and was rolling down the hill behind us. Hiro rested the butt of the .357 on top of the rock, squinting through the bullets and the flying rock chips.

The Dealership

"*Blam, blam.*" That .357 makes one terrible racket. Two rifles fell out of the car and clattered on the drive, followed by two dead guys lolling halfway out the doors. Lee stood and stared, his arms full of white plastic bags, and a stupid expression on his face.

Sally made what I think should be called an executive decision. She walked around the rock, .38 raised. "You shot Darren," she said. She shot Lee. I think she would have hit him right between the eyes, but he saw it coming. He threw the white plastic bags up in the air and ducked. Sally's bullet gave new meaning to the nickname *snow* for cocaine. The whole scene disappeared in a white fog, and when the fog cleared, Lee had roared around the parking lot in the Cadillac and was racing back down the lane.

We were all shooting at him. Both rear tires went flat, so did the right front, and there was no glass left in the windows, but Lee kept accelerating. He whipped behind the last lava rock. We heard a terrible screech when he sideswiped the limo, and then a breathless silence. That Cadillac arced gracefully up into the air and did a swan dive over the edge of the cliff. It was many silent heartbeats before we heard the crunch and saw a flash of flame from the explosion.

We changed our reservation at Duke's to a table for nine. They seated us outside, overlooking the beach and the pool. Betty, Maude, and I arrived first. Maggie, in a much more conservative, but still slinky dress, was right behind us. Next came Hiro, Sally, and Lani. Sally had flown to the Big Island, ridden up to Chun's with Hal, and hugged Lani while Hal snapped the cuffs on her stepmother. She brought Lani back to Oahu with her, and Lani looked pretty happy about that.

We'd already ordered our first round of drinks when George and Monica came in. That was my first look at Monica, and she did look like a movie star. In fact, she looked familiar, but I'm not going to admit to watching any porn flicks.

Maggie had ordered a bottle of Zinfandel and poured a lethal dose into Lani's water glass, circumventing the age problem. The two of them were cloistered, celebrating Maggie's dollar-an-hour raise.

The rest of us were celebrating the thirty-thousand-dollar reward from Crime Stoppers for busting the cocaine ring, and we were deducting that from Sally's bill.

The End